CRIMSON

Ten Tales of the Girl with the Red Hood

CLAIRE WARNER

Crimson
Short Story Compilation
Published by Raven Press

This is a work of fiction. Any similarity to any persons, living, dead or undead, is purely coincidental.

ISBN: 978-0-9954631-4-1 (Paperback Edition)

ALSO BY CLAIRE WARNER:

Night Flower:
The Black Lotus
Blood Orchid
Faded Rose (in progress)

Coils of Copper and Brass:
Amber Sky
Copper Temple (in progress)
Silver City (TBC)

Chronicles of Viridia:
Spell and Steel (TBC)

Well it's been a long road with this one. First conceived when I bought the pretty book cover (without a book to go with it) and worked on diligently until a data loss trashed half of the stories. This has been a labour of love for me and now it's finally ready. Within this book you will find stories about girls in sky cities of the future, girls who fight monsters and girls who exist at the edge of the solar system. I hope you love reading these tales as much as I enjoyed writing them.

CONTENTS

BLOOD ON SNOW

It was dusk and snow had finally begun to fall. The hunter hunched his shoulders against the drifting flakes and trudged through the forest, a brace of rabbits hanging over his shoulder. His breath blew out in soft clouds and chapped exposed skin. Despite the thickness of the trees, snow filled the air, obscuring his vision and making him feel nervous. A blizzard was on its way and he was still some distance from home. Pulling his hood even closer about his face, he picked up the pace, trudging doggedly onward, desperate for the light and warmth of his home.

Half a mile away, oblivious to the hunter's struggles, a pale figure drifted through the trees. Unlike the hunter she did not hide from the cold, as it did not bother her. Beneath clothes that seemed only to exist as modesty or decoration, skin the colour of ice glimmered in the dim light. Roses of ice clung to her breasts, their delicate traceries flowing across her skin as though they were a bodice, and a skirt of frosted spider webs danced about her legs. Snow slid against her bare arm, tickling the pale skin as the bitter winter wind whipped her long, silvery-white hair like a flag. In the dimming light, she was a pale ghost gliding amongst flurries of snow. As the sun disappeared behind the bare trees, she beckoned to the winter breeze. The drifting flakes called to her and she spun, directing the incoming blizzard to coat the landscape. The wind that so chilled the hunter welcomed her as a friend and she guided it to greater heights. Her hair tumbled in the gale and she danced along with it, following the storm to its destination.

A delighted giggle burst from her lips and she drifted down to the ground, her bare feet stepping onto the snow as lightly as a feather.

The hunter stumbled as the wind buffeted his fur-clad form. As the sun vanished the temperature dropped, the freezing gusts rising to a gale. The snow that had been steady but light now drove against his face and buried his path. Nervous, he shifted the weight of the rabbits and continued onwards, hoping to find some shelter before the storm brought down its full force. He wished he had not ventured deep into the wood but it could not be helped. Spring was late, the blizzards and frost continuing further into the year than usual and because of this, food was short. The pitiful rabbits that hung over his shoulder were the result of a full day's hunting. He took another step in the deepening snow, slowing down due to the difficult conditions. As he struggled through the building storm, he thought he heard laughter on the air but he shrugged off the speculation, mindful of the dangers of cold-induced fancy. He took another few paces as the blizzard gained in strength. The flakes obscured his vision and hid what was left of the path. Scared now, he raised his hands to protect his eyes as he trudged ahead, mindful of the fate of those who had been caught out in the storm before.

The blizzard carried her to the tops of the trees and she stared down at the whitening landscape with satisfaction. A solitary flake landed on her hand and she marvelled at the intricacy of its design. A delighted laugh echoed through the trees and she flew on, the snow crowning her head and shoulders as though it were a cape. A few moments later and she came to a halt. There was a figure below her, struggling to walk through the wind. She had seen these creatures before; she believed they were called humans. Fragile scraps of flesh and bone, helpless against the storms she drove. Most times she delighted in sending the gale against them but today she stopped; today she drifted closer. The flurries of snow whipped around his body as she peered at his face, intrigued by the ruddy colour to his skin.

The flakes bombarded his form but he kept going, forcing his feet one in front of the other. The little skin that was exposed to the elements felt numb and he dropped his hands to rearrange the scarf that covered his lips. His startled shout bounced off the trees as he stared directly at the face before him. Eyes like sapphires and hair the colour of snow sat above lips of dark violet. The shock made him stumble and he fell back against the nearest tree, blinking at the unnatural sight.

'You can see me?' Her voice was musical, like wind chimes in a high breeze.

The hunter nodded, almost unsure of what he heard.

The woman floated before him in a cloud of frost and snow and shivers raced over his body as the temperature dropped further. 'Who?' He couldn't say whether the shaking tones were due to fear or cold as they could be attributed to either.

She dropped to the ground, her feet landing silently in the snow bank. The man could see her and the strangeness of it drew her closer, for none other had been able to see what drove the blizzard. The hunter shuddered as her freezing aura surrounded him and stole his breath. In fascination she watched him, intrigued by his actions. His arms curled about his body, clutching the heavy coat tighter against his chest. She did not understand the attraction or his actions, yet something called her closer. A finger stretched towards his chilled face and he flinched away from the bitter chill. She smiled at the motion and drew her hand back.

'Who are you?' He spoke again, his voice tremulous, weak yet wondering. The strange face drifted closer to his; pale, pointed features that were strangely beautiful beneath a storm-cloud of silver-white hair. His eyes followed the rippling flow of her clothing with fear-tinged wonder.

'Geada.' Snow fell from her lips as she spoke. 'Who are you?' Curiosity laced each frost-laden word and he flinched away, his fingers turning numb at the deepening cold.

'Athan ...' The syllables were drawn out through trembling lips and he wondered if he were dying. This vision of bitterly cold beauty could not possibly be real. Snow filled the air between them and sapped his strength. Slumping back against the tree, he wrapped his arms about himself and tried to stay warm. Cold stole across his toes and he felt the incipient nip of frostbite.

'Athan.' Her fingers reached and tugged the hood from his head. Ruddy features spoke of the warmth that pumped beneath his skin. A finger of burning frost traced across his flesh in wonderment and she drew back her hand in surprise. 'It burns.' The sizzling heat sang in her flesh and called at her, making her reach forward for more of the sensation.

Athan felt her cold fingers about his skin and he began to panic. She was so cold that her touch seared his skin and drew the heat from him. This beautiful girl would be his death and she didn't seem to realise it. 'Please, Geada.' Tiredness seeped through him as he stretched out his gloved hands towards her. 'Please don't. Please let me live.'

'Live?' Inquisitive tones tinkled like shards of crystal as she quirked a silvery eyebrow. His flushed skin was becoming pale and his lips, once pink, were now deepening to blue.

'You're killing me,' He slumped back, the warmth fading as exhaustion plucked at his bones. 'I'll no longer breathe or move if you …' Shudders racked through him and he tried pull free but the cold seeping through him made him lethargic and weak.

Geada sat back and stared at the creature. The heat that so fascinated her seemed to be fading and as she watched he slipped deeper into a stupor. She pulled her hand from him and watched a little of his colour return. Memories of other humans who had frozen beneath her touch raced through her mind. It would be wrong to send Athan to sleep, for he could see her. Returning her hands to her side, she stepped backward and held back the bitter, winter wind that so harmed Athan's fragile form.

'Will you live now?'

Athan felt the bitter cold fall away and he tried to drag himself upright, but his chilled limbs refused to obey him. Falling back into the soft snow, his eyelids began to close. Thoughts of his family flashed through his mind as he tried to remain awake.

For a moment, Geada puzzled over his strange behaviour. The warmth in his body still flickered but it was weak and fading fast. Ordinarily she would have let the frost snuff the heat from his fragile frame, but that would not answer her question. Why could he see her? None of the other humans had. He was failing and this sight baffled her. With the strong wind buffeting at her back, she could hear the sounds of more humans battling through the snow. A decision was made and she returned to his side.

'Shout for help.' He lifted his head at her crystal voice. 'I will carry your words.'

Confused, but grateful for any help, Athan called out into the storm in a voice stripped of its usual vigour. Geada caught the wind easily and wrapped his voice within it before sending it out across the forest. Half a mile away, a trio of trappers heard the plaintive cry and began to move toward it. His voice spent and raw, Athan lay back and stared into her face, the chilling beauty holding his attention more than he would have thought possible.

'So beautiful,' he murmured, reaching out with a hand, almost forgetting her effect on his skin. 'So very beautiful ...' His hand dropped to the ground as he finally succumbed to deadly sleep that called to his body.

Panicking, Geada built up the wind behind the trackers, driving them into the clearing as though they were ships at

full sail. They gave a shout at the sight of Athan and rushed forward. Geada dropped the wind to a whisper as they focused on the stricken figure. She watched with concern as the group wrapped the young man in heavy blankets and began to carry him home.

'Do you see her?' Athan mumbled as they carted him away. 'Geada,'

The men glanced about the clearing and shook their heads, no doubt dismissing his words as hallucination brought on by the cold. But Athan kept his gaze on the beautiful maiden of ice and snow, all the way back to his home.

A longing settled into her bones as Geada watched the small group carry Athan through the trees. Careful to keep the snow from becoming too obvious, she drifted after the party, following them back to a large cabin deep in the heart of the forest. Entranced by the dwelling, she hovered above the clearing, the storm building as she watched the family rush to the doorstep and embrace him.

* * *

Several days passed and Athan finally left the bed in his small room. Frostbite had claimed one of his toes and a finger but he was awake and lucid. Dreams of Geada had haunted his dreams for those nights, a strange mix of longing and fear that left him moaning her name in the dark. He dressed in a set of warm clothing, stepped downstairs and headed for the kitchen. His mother and his sister Katherine pottered about the lit stove, a meagre yet warm stew bubbling on the hearth.

'Athan,' His sister gave him a hug and he returned it clumsily, still not fully recovered.

'I'm alright,' He answered, his words still slightly slurred with sleep. Stepping back from his sister, he picked up a cup of warmed wine and took a sip. 'I just need to warm up some more.'

'What happened?' His mother finished stirring the stew and turned to face him. 'The others said they found you in the woods, babbling about a young woman.'

'I thought I saw …' Athan hesitated, wondering how they would view his vision. Geada was an impossibility, a beautiful woman composed of snow and ice. They could think him mad. Tearing his eyes away from the rim of his cup, he stared into the curious eyes of his family. 'I thought I saw a woman out in the storm,' It was poor description for Geada. Despite her strange skin and hair, he felt drawn to her beauty with a physical ache that mystified him.

'Was she lost?' His sister questioned, ever practical and unimaginative. 'Did you help her?'

'She wasn't …' He grimaced, trying to work out how to put Geada into words. 'She was pale and so cold, almost like a ghost.' He looked at the liquid in his cup to avoid seeing the incredulous stare of his sister. 'She was no ghost but living.' He took a breath swamped by a sense of longing that raged through his bones. 'And so cold, like the blizzard itself.'

There was a crash as Athan's mother dropped one of the bowls she was carrying. Katherine and Athan exchanged a brief glance, before they both bent down to pick up the pieces of pottery.

'I'm sorry,' she breathed as they loaded the broken crockery into the bin. She moved the pan off the heat and sank into a chair with a sigh that spoke of pain. Athan looked at her pale face and something constricted in his chest.

'Mother?'

'A woman in the storm.' Her voice was hushed and scared. 'That seemed to be made of frost?'

'Yes.' He shook his head. 'I know it sounds mad …'

'She's a Winter Spirit.' His mother interrupted his rationalisation and Athan raised an eyebrow at her words. 'A Sprite belonging to Mother Winter.' A bitter, angry note flowed through her voice. 'And you saw her?' He nodded once more, not trusting his voice to speak.

'What's a Winter Spirit?' Katherine asked, her voice small and curious.

'A Winter Spirit controls Winter,' Their mother explained, a little more life entering her voice as she spoke. 'They direct the winds and frost.' She took a breath. 'They are as real as the snow they make fall.' She reached out for a cup of warm tea with shaking hands. She took a deep breath as though she feared the next words from her mouth. 'And if you see them, you are fated to die.'

Athan swallowed, unable to find a response to his mother's words. He recalled Geada's icy beauty with a pang and wondered if she had known his fate. Yet she had sent him home.

'Athan's not going to die,' Katherine announced with typical bravado. "He saw her and he's still here."

Their mother gave a weak smile and took a sip of tea. Athan was not fooled, he could see the glimmer of tears in his mother's eyes.

'This is ridiculous.' He fought down the fear with anger. 'Surely if that were the case, I would have died already.'

'They say that when a Winter Spirit is seen by a human, they become fascinated with them.' She reached up and drew aside the kitchen curtains. Outside, the blizzard pelted the small cabin, creating drifts of snow that piled against the windows. 'I think your spirit followed you back and is waiting outside for you to go to her.' A tear slid down her cheek. 'And you will eventually because that is your fate.'

Athan stared through the frosted glass and out into the storm. At first, he could see nothing beyond the falling snow. The white flew across the clearing like a curtain. 'There's nothing …' A flicker of movement in the air stalled his words. Geada. The spirit drifted near the trees and he stared hungrily at her form, her beauty capturing him once more. Almost without thinking, he reached for the window latch, only to have his hand slapped down by his mother.

'You'll go to her because that is her gift, to seduce those that see.' Pushing him back from the window, she dragged him next to the stove. 'Sit there and stay warm.' Nodding to Katherine, she continued. 'Make sure he stays there.' With several quick strides, she headed for the door and opened it. The cold blasted the small kitchen and Athan got to his feet, sensing Geada's chill presence before the door closed and his mother stepped into the snow.

Geada watched the woman with interest. Dressed in an apron and warm clothing, she was scarcely suited for her weather. Her face marked her as kin to Athan and Geada drifted closer, bringing a chill to the woman's skin.

'Leave my son alone,' the woman demanded, her voice close to tears as her gaze swept the clearing. 'You cannot have him.' A tear slipped from her eye and froze on her cheek. 'Find someone else.'

Confused, Geada brushed the glittering tear and stared at it in wonder.

'You'll kill him …' The rage and fear in her voice was undeniable.

Geada hesitated. She would not hurt Athan but he could see her and that meant … She did not know precisely what that meant, yet something sang within her bones and drew her ever closer.

Turning back from the woman, she focused on the wooden door. Wind whipped past her and threw the door open, blowing out candles and sending a freezing blast of air into the room. Athan was beside the stove and she stepped back from the heat, discomfited by the unnatural warmth.

'Geada,' She could sense the longing trapped beneath the fear in his voice and she moved closer, the cold fighting the warmth of the cabin.

'Athan.' Her hand reached out for him and he moved to stand but the slight girl beside him pinned him in place.

'No, Athan.' The girl's voice was fearful but strong and she held onto her brother with conviction. 'Don't leave.' Her eyes flickered about the cabin unsure of where Geada stood.

'Katherine, she won't hurt me,' Athan remembered the way she had directed the cold from him and called the rescuers. Despite what his mother said, he was convinced that Geada would try not to hurt him.

Katherine clearly believed differently and she pulled him backwards towards the fire. 'Get away from him.' Her fingers fumbled with the stove door and undid it. Geada stepped back as the warmth increased, pain lancing over her skin as her chilled flesh began to warm. Backing towards the door, she fled out into the snow.

'Kat,' Despite his injuries, Athan wrestled with his sister, throwing her aside and slamming the stove door. 'Geada!' He rushed towards the door and out into the snow, his feet sinking into the deep drifts as he did so. The cold whipped around him but he could still see her, hovering on the edge of the clearing.

'Athan, no,' His mother caught hold of his arm but he brushed her off as he moved across the clearing.

'Geada.' He stopped at the edge of the clearing and she drifted down to him. He did not know what he wanted, but his bones sang for it.

Geada drifted closer and laid a burningly cold hand against his cheek. Trembling, Athan leaned in and they kissed. Chill stole his breath as a gale of snow whipped about them. Geada struggled to rein in her cold as his fingers slid into her hair and drew her into his arms. His body-heat was burning her and she was wary of harming him. After several moments, she pushed herself away and he dropped to the ground, chilled from her touch.

'I'm sorry.' She drifted away and gave rein to her frustration in the deep emptiness of the woods. Snow and ice lanced through the glades, locking the forest into a cauldron of ice. She needed his touch and it was beyond her understanding. Those burning kisses had laced fire across her lips and she desired more.

* * *

It took a week this time for Athan to recover, his dreams filled with ice, snow and the beautiful girl that controlled them. His

mother kept him in bed, keeping him locked in the house and away from temptation. In lucid moments he knew that she was dangerous, but all that vanished with the memory of her kiss. His mother and Katherine kept watch on his locked bedroom door and they kept the fire high through the increasingly powerful gusts of wind. They had sealed the outer shutters to his room and in the dull candlelight he drifted between waking and sleeping. Reality and dreams mixed as he veered between anger and pleading.

Geada waited, her patience exhausted. The storm had raged for days and she still had not moved from her position in the glade. The family still watched and kept Athan from her. They had secured their windows against her winds and the chimney bellowed hot, dark smoke and kept her out. She knew she had other duties but she could not leave, kept outside his window, she was driven by emotions that she didn't understand. On the twelfth day, and frustrated beyond endurance, she acted. The ice crackled about her form and she grew an icicle from the eaves of the cottage itself, a spear of ice the thickness of a man's leg and the weight of a young calf. With a scream of pure rage, she hurled at the house and the barricaded window that she knew to be his.

The boards and glass shattered as the icicle smashed through. Athan watched with a mixture of fear and excitement as shards of glass and wood sprayed the room. The wind screamed through the newly opened aperture, chilling the room to the temperature outside. Expectation flared and he stood up, pushing the heavy covers away as he watched the open window. Snow blew in through the wrecked frame and gusted about the room in dancing patterns of white.

'Athan.' His mother shouted from the other room as she pushed at his door, while Geada appeared at the window and gale-force winds flooded the room to slam the door shut. 'No, please ...'

Athan heard his mother's anguished cry for help but he paid it no heed, his eyes and attention were fixed on the window and Geada. Bitter winds wrapped about him and propelled him from beside the bed to her waiting arms. She carried him through the window and out into the white landscape beyond. The cold blistered against his skin but he did not care, too caught up in the spell of her.

* * *

Behind them, his mother's distant cries echoed into the howling wind as Athan's senses were dulled and overwhelmed by the arms that held him. They travelled deep into the forest for a mile, two miles from the cottage and she finally stopped, carefully placing him in a drift of freezing snow. She hovered above him for a moment, the storm dying about them as she reached forward, her fingers trailing across his skin, burning with their chill.

'You ...' Her voice was a whisper of wonder and need. A need that Athan recognised even as his flesh chilled beneath her touch.

'I ...' The words could not come and she fell forward her lips capturing his in a blistering kiss of frost and fire.

Athan lost his senses as her kisses seared against him. Driven by something primal, he felt his clothes tear from his body as she trailed her bitter lips against his. He reached up an arm and crushed her against him, dragging the frost-rimmed fabric free. Pain and pleasure, he could no longer tell which as her body moved against his. He was under the spell of a passion he did not understand as her flimsy garments of ice disappeared beneath his touch. The cold sank into his bones as the passion soared through him burying himself into her embrace as they moved as one.

'Geada,' he groaned as they drew apart, passion finally spent. As he struggled to lift his head his own thoughts returned, freed from whatever madness had held them captive. 'I … I'm …' He could not even lift his hand to touch her frozen skin. Darkness flickered at the edges of his vision and he felt himself drift down into a slumber that promised to be endless. As the darkness descended, his last thoughts were of his mother and the warning that she had tried so hard to impart.

And if you see them, you are fated to die

* * *

'Athan …' Geada stepped back from his cold form, her body burning with the life she had quenched, and howled at the sky. The desire that had seared them faded, leaving her hollow and alone All that was left was a body, rapidly chilling in the cold, white snow. 'Why could I not stop?'

'Destiny, dear one.' Her head snapped up and she stared at the shimmering face above her.

'Mother Winter.' She bowed her head, crystal tears sliding to the ground. 'I killed him.' Frosted tears dripped onto his pale skin and she reached a hand to them, realising that for the first time his heat did not burn her.

'You did.' Mother Winter reached down and cupped her

face. 'You were fated and neither of you could stop that.' A hand reached down and pressed against her abdomen. 'For what you did will bring forth life.' Geada felt a flickering warmth beneath her skin and she stared up at the icy eyes above her. 'Born of passion, ice and fire …' Her gaze drifted to the body in the snow. 'A girl of blood.' Hands retrieved her hooded cape and placed it about Geada's shoulders. 'And Spring …'

Fire seared through Geada's veins as the flickering sensation burst into life and then gasped at the warmth that streaked through her flesh.

'I don't …' A jolt of heat left her gasping as her body grew hotter than she had ever known it to be.

'You were my chosen for Spring.' A smile creased Mother Winter's lips as she indicated the still form beneath them. 'He was fated as yours.'

'But I …'

'Why do you think you desired so much?' Mother Winter covered the body in a blanket of snow. 'This was your task.'

'But I didn't want to kill him …' Soft entreaty flowed through her voice. 'I never wanted to …'

'You had to.' Mother Winter placed a chill hand against her body and Geada flinched feeling the cold for the first time.

The cape around her shoulders trembled against her skin as it changed colour from white to deepest red. The hood settled against hair of the palest green and a new set of clothing wreathed her form. Still the colour of ice but with hints of green, the dress felt strange, as warm as Athan's lips. She glanced back at the shrouded form and bit her lips.

'Now, my girl,' Mother Winter smiled at her. 'Go out and bring in Spring.'

Casting one lingering look back at Athan, Geada took to the air and began to drift between the trees feeling the warmth of Spring suffuse the landscape. The snowy forest beckoned and she continued on, drawing forth the dormant life from the soil and replacing the icy winds with warmer ones.

The bitter breeze lifted and life began to return to the barren soil. Her once white gown was now green and covered with blossom and she coaxed the life back to the world as the fluttering in her abdomen quickened with the rising temperature.

The life within her grew swiftly, far swifter than mortal life, mirroring the change of the season. As the frost and snow melted from the forest floor and the last bits of winter rolled back, she brought forth a daughter. Dark-haired and ruddy with Athan's life stamped throughout. As the snow melted beneath her feet, Geada carried the small bundle to the last snow-bank and Athan. With sorrow she sat beside him and finally called to Mother Winter.

'Can I give my heat back to him?' She asked, flinching away from the chill that emanated from the spirit. Her eyes traced his form and she swallowed a tear. 'For it is my fault he lost it.'

Mother Winter looked over at her and a small smile graced her lips. 'He has not fully gone.'

Elated, Geada placed the child on the ground and removed the last of the frozen shroud. As the final bits of snow melted, Athan was revealed, supine against the ground as though he were sleeping. Geada called to the life bursting within her and placed her hands against his chest. The warmth of the new season seared through her and found the small kernel of life that still pulsed deep within him. As the life within her warmed him she felt her own slipping away. As the flush of life returned to his cheeks the last of her warmth fled returning her to the cold state she was before.

The dress of green and blossom faded to white and as the frost bloomed once again across her skin, she wrapped the cape about her daughter. She knew he would take care of her. With one last lingering look at the slumbering man, she faded into the sky to await the next winter.

* * *

Athan woke to the feel of mud and the warmth usually associated with Spring. Confused he sat up and stared about the clearing. The snowy, freezing landscape had vanished and in its place was the muddy slush associated with the thaw. As a warmer breeze tousled his hair, the gurgling cry of a baby drew his startled attention. A bundle of red fabric wriggled against his thigh and he stared down at it with surprise. He didn't remember a baby. He searched his thoughts, struggling to recall what had happened prior to his eyes opening to this thaw.

'Geada!' He started upright and called into the trees bewildered by the sense of loss that engulfed him. 'Geada!' The baby fussed and he reached down to lift it from the wet ground. He peeled back the cape and stared down at pale blue eyes beneath dark hair, Geada's eyes. He stilled, the impact of the babe's appearance rushing through his mind like a torrent. 'Is this ours?' He received no answer from the clearing. The babe lifted a finger and pressed it against his face. Athan stayed for a long moment before he reached down and searched for his clothes. As he dressed, his eyes kept returning to the baby

and the features that marked her as his.

'I'll look after our daughter,' he whispered as, with one last look about the clearing, he cradled his burden and returned home. The small house stood as he had left it, though new shutters now covered the window to his room.

'Athan?' He looked up as his mother rushed out of the front door 'My Athan!' Tears rolled down her cheeks as she drew him into her arms. 'I thought she had …' She glanced fearfully about the clearing as though expecting to see Geada lurking in the corner.

'It's alright, Mother. She's gone,' Athan said, sorrow rippling through him for the loss.

'Is that …?' She pointed at the baby in his arms and raised an eyebrow.

'He looked down at the baby, searching her face and seeing his own and her mother's features stare back at him. His face creased into a wondering smile. 'I think I'll call her Rose.'

CRIMSON

'Ma!' The girl in the red hood slipped and fell heavily as she ran through slushy, melting snow. Picking herself up from the cold, wet ground she continued to run, shouting as she moved. 'Ma!' She broke free from the treeline and rushed toward the cottage, lungs burning with effort as she forced more speed from her tired legs. Reaching the heavy wooden door, she fumbled hastily with the latch and nearly fell over the step in her eagerness to cross the threshold.

'What is it, Mina?' Her mother came out of the kitchen, hands floured from baking and stared down at her daughter.

'There's been a death in the village.' Her daughter gulped out, breath almost gone from her exertions.

'And?' Her mother rubbed her hands clean on her apron and pushed the door shut, stopping the heat from escaping.

'They're saying that one of the Taken did it.'

A flash of horror lit her mother's eyes and she turned to the locked cupboard that lay beside the door. Within there was a brigandine breastplate, gauntlets and greaves. Removing her apron, she began to dress. A padded shirt went on first, followed by the armour with the pair of thick gauntlets and set of greaves. She tied a chainmail choker about her throat and reached back into the cupboard for her weapons. A long, razor-sharp knife of purest silver went into a boot scabbard and several small vials came to rest in a bandoleer that criss-crossed her chest. Sliding a longer sword into the scabbard she reached back into the cupboard and removed a heavy crossbow fitted with two strings for rapid firing.

'Can I come with you, Ma?' Mina asked, watching her mother with undisguised envy. 'You said I needed experience.'

'Not today.' her mother answered as she began tying a quiver to her back. "You're still too young." She checked the fastenings once more before reaching back into the cupboard and drawing out a long scarlet cape, its colour designed to be seen against the monochrome colours of the forest. Mina had asked the reason for the colour when she was younger and her mother had explained that they were not hunters or scouts, but killers who didn't need to hide. Fastening the clasp at her throat, her mother turned back to the door and unlatched it. Flurries of snow blew across the threshold as her mother bent her head and kissed her daughter on the cheek.

'Remember, the Taken are not always the enemy,' she whispered before she turned back to the door. Drawing the hood about her head, she stepped to the threshold 'The vow is everything,' she whispered before she stepped down out of the cottage and into the whirling snow beyond.

Mina waited till the fiery fingers of dawn tinted the eastern sky for signs of her mother's return. All through the preparation of breakfast she stayed ready, with one eye on the clock that sat on the mantle. As lunchtime drew near and the uneaten breakfast still lay on the scrubbed wooden table, she knew that her mother would not return.

When the village Elder visited as the late afternoon sun began to dip in the West, she nodded blankly as he coldly informed her of her mother's death. She had killed the Taken, but she had given the last of her heart's blood to the snowy forest floor. In accordance with the oath, he built the pyre and placed her mother's body on it while Mina was the one to touch the faggots with flame and watch her mother's body transform into fire. As the Elder offered her a place in his home, she set her lips and shook her head.

With the scarlet cape, the ashes of her mother and her weapons, Mina travelled to the citadel and pledged herself to a life of combat.

* * *

The houses lining the dirt road were familiar, as was the white-washed town hall. Mina strode along the path, conscious of the eyes that watched her. The scarlet cape covered her but did not hide the weapons that lay at her belt and across her back. Her dark hair was neatly braided and her skin marked with fine scars, the history of her chosen path written in each line.

'Welcome.' The Elder strode from his residence to meet her with a smile that didn't reach his eyes. 'We welcome the Chosen to our village.'

'And I offer my blade in your protection.' The words were

ritualistic, of a tradition that reached far back in history. She removed the dagger at her belt and held it out. 'This blade is my oath.'

'And we hold your oath sacred.' A moment, a stillness of breath and the promise was made. As the Elder's words died, Mina felt the crowd gather at her back. Whispers swirled about her and she wondered at their tone. The arrival of a Chosen was normally a time for relief or joy. At the least there would be respect or awe but the mood of the crowd was strange, almost unwelcoming. The Elder had said the official words but …

'I don't know why you've come.' The Elder's words cut through her thoughts and she took a breath. Unwelcome was right, the Elder's greeting had all the warmth of frost and prickles raced along the back of her neck. 'You are not needed here, Chosen.'

Mina returned the blade to her belt and took a moment before answering. The crowd behind her shifted and tension licked across her flesh as muttering could be heard.

'I was called to deal with the Taken in the Western Wood.' Her voice was mild and leeched of emotion. The Chosen were not given to displays of passion or feeling and her training had been exemplary in that regard.

'You have a writ?'

The request to see the writ was unusual. It was enough that a Chosen arrived. However, such a thing could be asked for. She reached into a pocket and drew out the sheaf of parchment. The Elder took the paper and read the words with a stillness that caused her concern.

'The warrant is clear.' The Elder raised his voice and

announced to the crowd. 'Welcome, Chosen.'

'I am Mina.'

'Kay's daughter?' A voice called from behind her and she turned. A woman in a baker's apron pushed through the crowd. 'We wondered what had happened to you.' She reached Mina's side and her eyes took in the armour and cloak with concern. 'You took the vow?'

'I took the vow.' She stepped back and controlled the rush of emotion that threatened her much-vaunted control. 'These ten years past.'

'Your mother's cottage still lies empty.' The woman half reached out a hand but thought better of it. 'We'll prepare it for you.'

'Thank you.'

'Your mother …' The baker swallowed the words and stepped back. 'Do you require nourishment?'

'I'll take some rest after I've spoken with the Elder.' Her eyes snapped back to the older man, curious as to why she did not recognise him. Though it had been ten years since she had last seen the council and it was likely that people could have died in the interim.

'Then I shall host you.' The smile was false and pasted on like a mask. Untrustworthy and possible dangerous. Mina weighed the options and nodded with the faint hint of a smile. Best that he thought she was unaware of his feelings.

'With pleasure.' She held out a hand. 'Lead on.'

He led her into the dim cool of his home. The shabby hallway led into an equally worn sitting room. He did not ask her to sit.

'Who called you?' Mina raised her eyebrow at the snap to

his voice. 'Why are you here?'

'There was a report of a slaying.' She reached into her bag and drew out the sheaf of paper. 'A lonely farmhouse and one family.' The Elder reached out tentative fingers but didn't take the paper. 'It was one of the Taken, so I was sent.'

'I see.' His mouth worked soundlessly for a moment before he forced a smile. 'Then you are welcome. Be well.' He showed her to the door and back out into the street.

As the door closed behind her, Mina strode into the familiar street sure of only one thing – the Taken was not the danger here.

* * *

The afternoon that followed felt calm but strange. Her questions were rebuffed and people avoided her on the street. The treatment was beyond trepidation, it bordered on hostile, and that bothered her. Her mother had never been shunned for her role and for a Chosen to be slighted so was beyond the pale. She spent her first night combing the woods for signs of the Taken and the next morning she visited her home. It was difficult.

Each part of her mother's house scoured her soul with memories. By the middle of the day, she decided to trek to the location of the massacre. Moving with the ease of long training, she soon vanished into the woods.

The trek wasn't hard and she arrived at the farmstead by mid-afternoon. The sun was high yet still the farm had the feel of shadows. She entered the main room and knelt at the mess of blood and spoor.

'Why are they lying to me?' A whisper in the stillness of

the house. Signs of the Taken were all over the house. She unloosened her crossbow and readied the string. It was too quiet here and that could not be laid at the usual hush that violent death generated. Moving around the small rooms she headed to the window and stared out at the lush forest. It was still, a quiet born of fear and trepidation. She loaded the crossbow and carefully searched her surroundings.

She turned from the window to continue searching the room. The scuff of a boot against the floor drew her attention bare seconds before a figure entered the room. She fired, the bolt slamming into flesh with a thud. The yell was masculine and she walked forward arming another bolt as she did so.

'Don't kill me.' The man huddled back against the wall, blood pouring from his side. 'I didn't …'

'Who are you?' Mina made no move towards him, knowing all too well the capacity of the Taken to deceive.

'Jakob.' The words stuttered out as fresh crimson blood leaked between his fingers. 'Please, help me …'

'What are you doing here?' Mina kept the crossbow trained on him as her eyes flickered around the room. Far too many memories of sympathy-induced traps kept her from aiding the stricken man. 'In this place of death.'

'The Elder wanted me to wait for you here.' His words stuttered out. 'I didn't mean to …'

'Why?' Her tone was pitiless in the face of his torment.

'He doesn't want you here.' More of his life-blood leaked to the dusty floor. 'He wants you gone.'

'Were you here to kill me?'

'I …' Panic crossed his face. 'I … wasn't … I …' Mina heard the truth in his stuttered protestations and anger settled into her bones. She fitted another bolt to the second string of the crossbow.

'Chosen?' The name was called from outside. 'Are you injured?' False concern echoed through the room.

'Don't answer.' Jakob whispered. 'He'll know I failed.'

Mina moved slowly to the window and, using the mirror she always carried, stared out into the courtyard. The Elder stood there flanked by his brothers and again the feeling of disquiet flooded her mind.

'He's one of them.' Her words were quiet but they reached the man on the floor with the clarity of a bell. 'But I don't understand … how could he be?' The Taken weren't usually so human. In all her experience, the Taken were more monster than man.

'I don't want to see you hurt, Mina.' The mirror showed him walking closer. 'I promised your mother that I wouldn't see you hurt.'

Mina dropped the mirror as realisation seared through her mind. Her mother's death and the Elder who had brought the news. Memories long lost ripped through her mind as she finally remembered his face and the blood that she had initially attributed to him carrying her mother's body. The shattering of the mirror galvanised the trio outside and, in an instant, they had shed the familiar, comforting form of humanity.

Setting her teeth Mina faced the window and fired, the bolt killing one of the beasts instantly as the other two leapt through the glass.

Dropping the crossbow, she drew the slender silver blade that she kept for close combat and met their charge. She didn't try to block, knowing that to do so would slam her to the floor or into a wall. Instead, the silver blade danced in the air aiming for an artery as she weaved away from clumsy, over-confident blows. One mistake from her enemy and dark, rich blood sprayed across her face. The silver cut deep and would keep the wound from closing, the resulting blood loss slowing him down.

The Elder snarled as his companion's blood bathed the room. Claws like daggers raked through the air and rent her armour. She couldn't help the scream of pain as they dug into her flesh and tore long shreds in the skin.

Ducking from the next blow, she reversed the blade and several dancing strikes cut at the arms and legs of her attacker, the razor-sharp edge slicing easily through fur and drawing blood.

The first Taken aimed a clumsy blow to her head and she staggered with the force. The Elder's teeth pulled back in vicious smile as he used her lack of balance to press the advantage. Mina screamed again as the claws raked across her back. A snarl creased her lips and she launched herself forward, seizing hold of the first Taken's arm and using his momentum to propel herself towards the Elder. Once, twice, the blade cut deeply into his chest causing the Elder to stagger back. Emboldened she continued the offensive, the silver weapon dealing myriad cuts to his arms and chest. Behind her the other Taken stumbled and fell, succumbing finally to blood loss.

'This is my town, Chosen,' the Elder snarled. 'It has been my town since before you drew breath.' Another claw tore into her leg and she bit back the cry forcing herself to continue. 'I have the power of life and death here.'

'You killed my mother.'

'Of course.' His fingers gripped her sword arm and applied pressure. 'I made one mistake and killed in error. She came for me. I couldn't let her take what I had built.'

Mina felt the strength in his hands but she refused to release the weapon. He would have to tear her arm off to make her drop it.

'And then you left and I thought I had control of this town. For ten years I've been the Elder here, building my family.'

Mina's thoughts flashed to her welcome only yesterday. How many had he tainted during his tenure?

'And this family?' She pushed aside the speculation as she pushed for an opening that would allow her to break free.

'Fools all of them.' The snarl was barely human as a maw of razor-sharp teeth clicked close to her face. 'Blackmailing me with you people.'

His other hand went for her throat but that small shift of weight was all she needed. Her muscles screamed as she jerked her feet upwards and slammed them against his chest. Mina used the upward motion to kick him in the chin. The Elder's fingers jerked open releasing her and she fell back in an inelegant roll. Grateful for the years of acrobatic training at the academy, Mina rolled into a crouch and waited.

The Elder rushed at her, the move that all Taken too far gone with anger fall prey to. In a heartbeat, Mina turned and slashed towards his open throat. The blade ripped open the artery and he staggered forward, shock over his features as he fell face down to bleed out against the ground.

Mina pulled herself upright and glanced about her. Both Taken were dead and the would-be assassin was close to it.

Before she turned to treat the man's wounds she reached into a pouch and dropped her mother's symbol onto the Elder's body. As the silver charm burnt into his flesh a tear fell down her face as she finally mourned.

RAZOR

'Rosa!'

The crowd turned to look as the shout echoed across the busy intersection. Several citizens whispered at the sight of the girl's ice-blue hair as she rushed past. Rosa watched with a smile as the fine-boned figure easily dodged the crowd to reach her.

'There you are,' she announced as she slowed to walk.

'Where else would I be?' Rosa smiled at her friend's enthusiasm. Hela was a Sprite and her gregarious personality coloured everything she did. The ice-blue hair, styled in a short pixie cut was an indication of this. Rosa's hair was less vibrant and she kept her natural colour of mousey brown.

'I don't know. The library, the gym ...?' A smirk lifted Hela's lips. 'Taking dancing lessons from Gino?'

'And giving Aunt Tirry heart failure. You do remember

what happened when I dyed my hair pink that time?' She affected a scolding tone. 'Vibrant hair colour is for Sprites and children, and you are neither.' A sigh escaped Rosa's lips. 'I thought she was going to faint.'

'There's nothing wrong with being a Sprite,' Hela responded with only the mildest dose of heat. She was used to the whispers and condemnation. 'Where on earth would she get her dose of entertainment without us?'

'I know. But you know what she's like.'

'Do I ever.' Hela rolled her eyes. 'Remember when we first became friends?'

'She wasn't happy.' Rosa's thoughts drifted back to Hela's first visit to her Aunt's small apartment. Aunt Tirry was an Engineer and not known for lightness or laughter. 'But I think she got used to it.'

Hela didn't answer, as though she didn't agree with her friend's hypothesis and Rosa didn't press, knowing that her aunt had never fully accepted the blue-haired girl at her home. Aunt Tirry was a senior Engineer and expectations for her behaviour were higher than it was for others. Her mother wouldn't have cared but she had died when Rosa was very young.

'Have you been to the wall yet?' Hela's voice broke into her thoughts and reminded her of another concern.

'No,' Rosa had been on her way to the wall, but slowly. The results of their final range of tests had finally been posted, complete with the details of their future careers. Hela had no worries about the tests, her future was set. Rosa's, on the other hand, was not as clear cut. She had tested highly for the engineering career, but she had also received high scores in several others, which would mean she would have to choose and that was something she did not wish to do.

'Well, let's go then.'

Hela grabbed hold of her arm and they walked through the crowd towards the Learning Centre. Set on the one hundred and twentieth floor of the Charter Building and linked by a sky bridge, travel to the Learning Centre was a nerve-wracking experience, particularly for Rosa, who suffered from vertigo. The doors from the Central Concourse opened onto a wide and graceful bridge. Rosa took a step across the threshold and swallowed nervously.

'Are you okay?' Hela caught hold of Rosa's arm and began to guide her across the expanse. Beneath them Rosa could see the thick smog that wreathed the lower floors and she took a steadying breath. 'Just one step in front of the other.' Hela's voice coaxed her as she tried not to think of the space below her.

With relief she stepped into the atrium of the Learning Annex and walked past the reception desk. The career wall was at the back and they headed straight for it, passing fellow students in various stages of emotion.

Across the wide, crisp expanse, lists of names scrolled endlessly, waiting for a command. Swallowing nervously, Rosa stepped forward.

"Student ID 20035678," she announced, grateful that her voice barely held a tremor. The screen stopped scrolling and her name flickered into existence. Leaning forward, she read the details and froze.

'What did you get?' Hela looked over her shoulder and gave a small whistle. 'Transfer Order Twelve?' She glanced across at Rosa, who was struggling to hold in her confusion 'How?'

'What's Transfer Order Twelve?' Rosa murmured as she re-read the instruction. 'I've never heard of it.'

All of the other transfer orders were known to her. One was Military, two was Governance and three medical. Had she been given the role of Engineer, then that would have been a four. But twelve was an unknown quantity. She glanced back at Hela and worried at the shock she saw on her face.

'Do you know?' she asked her friend. Hela shifted slightly and a pained expression creased her features. 'Well?' Rosa demanded.

'I don't really know anything. I …' Hela glanced across the crowd. 'It's rare. It's …' She caught hold of Rosa's arm and leant closer. 'It's military and dangerous, people don't usually talk about it but …'

'Rosa Lunswick?' A man's voice cut across Hela's hurried tones and she looked up. A soldier strode into view and Rosa's stomach sunk like a stone. The military were rarely seen on these levels of the city. 'I'm here to take you to your new home.'

'But my aunt …' Rosa protested as she stared up at him, shock and fear making her voice squeak.

'Will have been informed.' He held out his arm and pointed towards the aircar that lay docked on the skycourse. 'Please.'

Casting a pleading look back over her shoulder at Hela, Rosa walked towards the car and got inside. The soldier sat on the seat opposite and with the barest whisper of noise, the car lifted into the air and they began to fly.

* * *

Quiet settled on the pair as Rosa sat, her fingers nervously twisted into her lap. As the car rose to cruising altitude, she regarded the man opposite her with increasing curiosity. His body was lean and well-muscled beneath the uniform of the Protectorate. She moved her eyes to his face and almost forgot to breathe. He was devastatingly handsome. Hazel eyes regarded her from an elegantly sculptured face and short, tawny-coloured hair crowned his head. As she struggled to keep her eyes in her head, he gave a small smile, as though he knew what she was thinking.

'What's your name? she asked, struggling to keep her mind on more mundane thoughts.

'Lieutenant Ren.'

'Do you know what …?' She stuttered to a halt as he shook his head.

'All I know is your assignment.'

'But isn't this unusual?' she asked, her voice rapid with nerves. 'I mean, don't I usually get orientation?'

'Transfer Order Twelve,' he replied. 'This is your orientation.'

Rosa settled back against the seat trying to remember the different orders. Transfer Order One usually sent people to careers in medical, or military circles. After several moments' thought, she turned back to Ren.

'So, if this is my orientation, you can tell me about it.'

An approving smile crept across his face. 'Well done,' he said, before reaching into a pocket, and drawing forth a tablet. 'One minute, thirty seconds.'

'What?'

'The time it took to realise your options.' He entered a

couple of details into the pad. 'Hold up your chip.'

Used as she was to requests from authority, she held out her right hand, and presented it to Ren.

'Submissive,' he noted, making another note on the sleek piece of apparatus before him. Colouring from his description of her, Rosa shrank back against the seat, and fell silent.

In the quiet plushness of the aircar, the only sound came from the gentle tapping of fingers on plastic. Unsure, and unnerved by the whole affair, Rosa turned her attention back to the window.

'We're heading to the lower level,' she squeaked, noting the increasing pollution with a wary eye.

'Can't get anything past you,' Ren noted, making her flush for the second time. 'Our destination is a training post on the ground.'

'The ground?' Rosa looked out at the thickening clouds with increasing trepidation. The ground was off-limits to most of the citizenship, the heavy pollutants in the low-lying smog and poison in the soil, rendered anything below level twenty unliveable. 'But I thought–' She paused, watching as his stylus moved once more across the tablet's surface.

'Yes?' He quirked an eyebrow, inviting her to continue.

'I thought the surface was poison.'

'It is.'

The aircar dropped below level twenty. The smog surrounding the vehicle had a sickly brown tinge to it. Rosa nervously wet her lips.

'So why am I going to the ground?' She couldn't help the quaver that entered her voice. 'Won't that kill me?'

Ren rested the tablet on his knee before he leaned forward.

'We'll see,' he replied, that strange, small smile still resting on his lips.

Level ten passed the window and Rosa clenched her fists. 'How has this anything to do with my orientation?' she demanded, panic making her voice hoarse. She took several deep breaths as Ren placed another note on his tablet. 'And what are you making notes on?'

'This particular note,' he waved the tablet at her. 'States that you become antagonistic when frightened.' A soft thump, as the aircar landed, prevented Rosa from answering. The door slid open and Ren pointed to the yawning, open doorway. 'Get out.'

Rosa froze, staring out into the gloom with unrestrained fear. Another note on the pad and he leant forward.

'I gave you an instruction.' A crisp almost harsh note of command entered his voice.

'I guess I'm not as submissive as you think,' Rosa snapped back before clamping her mouth shut in shock.

'If you don't get out of the car under your own will,' he continued as though he hadn't heard. 'I will enter you for processing.'

Rosa heard the finality in his voice, and she swallowed. Processing meant scrapping of your current career path and a potential reduction in living grade. She had heard of former students permanently sent to the service grades on level thirty. Tentatively, she scooted to the edge of the seat, and gingerly placed her legs out of the car. A warm, clammy mist gusted across her skin and she took a breath. The air was thick, heavy with several different scents, none of them pleasant and she clamped her mouth shut, hesitant to suck in any more of the polluted smog.

'Go on.'

She felt his hand on the small of her back as he pushed her out of the car. Her palms landed in the pitted and cracked concrete slicing several small cuts into the skin. As she picked herself upright, she heard the sound of the aircar door closing. Turning to face the vehicle, she caught sight of Ren's face. The smirk was gone, leaving an impassive mask in its place. The tablet was still in his hand, but as she watched, he lifted a finger and pointed down the street.

Nervously, she moved off in the direction he was pointing. Above her, the buildings vanished into the fog. There were no windows at this level, and she could see why. Visibility was almost at zero, and there was nothing green. The concrete beneath her feet was ancient and pebble-dashed with loose stones, only greyish fungi grew between the numerous cracks. The sun didn't penetrate to this level, and the gloom was oppressive.

A growl sounded from up ahead and she froze, her heartrate increasing as she focused on the noises that were approaching on all sides.

She glanced back to the aircar and almost cried out. It was no longer parked on the pitted floor. The sleek vehicle had vanished, leaving her alone.

'Wait!' She started to run back when a creature barrelled out of the darkness. A claw sliced through her upper thigh, sending her to the ground. A screech of pain escaped her lips, as she stared up at the beast that now advanced on her prone form. Half the size of the aircar, the thing was covered in thick, shaggy fur. Blood dripped from its claws and mouth.

'Help!' She scooted back on her hands slicing more cuts in the already lacerated skin. The creature moved forward, stalking her frantically-moving body. A clang sounded in the ruined alley, as her reaching fingers knocked a metal pipe across the ground. Petrified and desperate, she reached for the long metal bar. Her fingers curled around the cold metal, and she stood, facing down the creature with a confidence she did not feel. The creature gave her a contemptuous look and stalked closer.

Rosa struck out with the weapon, the steel bar bouncing harmlessly off the thick fur. The creature snarled in response, and lashed out for the second time. The bar hit the ground, ripped from her hands with one powerful blow. Backing up, her back hit the solid bulk of a wall and she froze. The creature moved in, and she screamed, holding her hands up in a defensive posture.

As the creature pounced, something clicked into place within her, a sensation of blistering energy that obliterated her panic. She dived to the side, the creature slamming into the wall. Only mildly dazed by the impact, the creature turned towards her, as a burning torrent of power unlocked the darkest recesses of her mind.

'No.' Her hand opened, a focus for all the power that had flared into being. As crackling blue sparks spilled from her hand and wreathed its shaggy form, the creature yelped in pain.

Stunned by the energies pouring forth, Rosa sank back against the wall, the light dying almost immediately. As the sparks faded, the creature recovered. Terrified once more, Rosa shrank away, trying to find the raw energy that had just saved her. A claw flashed out and sliced deeply across her upper arm and she screamed as her blood sprayed across the street.

The same energy flared out of her again like the sun and the scent of burning flesh rose from the creature's skin though it still staggered towards her. Pressed against the wall, Rosa felt her knees buckle as a wave of tiredness swept through her. The rough concrete grated against her back as she slid to the ground, her eyes darkening, the blue, crackling energy dimmed to a flicker as she finally faded into unconsciousness.

* * *

She woke in a darkness so complete she had to check if her eyes were open. The softness of a bed cocooned her frame and a light sheet covered her. Pushing herself upright she stared blindly about, confused that the room's sensors hadn't triggered with her movement and illuminated the space.

'Lights,' The room remained dark. 'Lights,' she called again, prickles of fear reasserting itself. Memories of the creature flooded through her mind and she suppressed a whimper. What was that creature and how had she managed to hurt it? 'Please, can you put on the lights?'

She pushed the sheet aside, and reached for the side of the bed. Carefully she dangled her legs over the edge, reaching for the solid familiarity of a floor; a floor that didn't seem to be there. She backed up and settled into what she assumed to be the centre of the bed. The darkness suffocated and pressed against her, provoking a fear that she barely understood.

'Please.' Tears pricked the back of her eyelids as she rolled into a foetal position. 'I don't know what's going on.'

Hugging her knees to her chest, her mind ran over the

events of that afternoon. It seemed like some nightmare yet she had not woken from it. Her thoughts went back to that morning's breakfast and Aunt Tirry commenting on her lack of passion for the engineering career. At the time she had airily waved away her aunt's concerns but now she would have given anything to be back in her kitchen.

Hela's worried face flashed into her thoughts. She had known about Transfer Order Twelve; she had been trying to tell her about it before Ren had whisked her away …

Ren … She took another breath as she focused on her memory of his mockingly handsome face and the comments he had added to her file.

Submissive. A small blaze of anger rushed through her at his description and she angrily wiped the tears that were sliding down her cheek away.

'I'll show you submissive,' she hissed into the empty darkness as her thoughts turned back to her encounter on the ground and the strange energy that had burned through her.

That energy was light. If she hadn't imagined it then she could call it and at least then she could see. She took another breath to steady herself and she reached inward for the strange, flickering spark that had burned into life. Long, slow breaths filled her lungs as the spark crackled through her body and rippled across her skin. Elusive and teasing the glow skittered away from her, leaving her once more in the dark. Swallowing back a fresh wave of tears she clenched her fists and forced the panic away from her. The spark flowed easier, the flickering energy crackling into sporadic, weak life. And this time it stayed.

The light surrounded and warmed her, pale bluish sparks

flaring across her skin to light the deep darkness.

'Well done.' Ren's rich voice cut through the room startling her. The light about her died, but not before she caught a glimpse of the space about her. The room was large, but not so big that she couldn't see the walls.

'What do you want? she called, hoping that her voice didn't tremble. 'What the hell is all this about?' She tried reaching for the light again but it eluded her call.

'All will be explained.' His voice continued in calm, orderly tones. 'All you need to know now is that Transfer Order Twelve has been confirmed.'

'No. You don't get to just dump me on the ground, leave me to face a monster and then leave me in the dark.' Outrage and fury fuelled her voice and sparks of electric blue fire rippled across her skin. 'Tell me what is going on right now or I swear I'll …'

Shutters rolled open, spilling bright sunlight into the room and the sparks on her skin faded into nothing.

Now that the room was bathed in bright sunshine it seemed friendlier, less oppressive than before. The king-size bed lay in the centre of the room and a set of double-doors were on the wall to her right.

'Well?' Slightly mollified by the gift of light but unwilling to forget the terror of her trip to the ground, Rosa posed her question to the empty air with an angry shrug of her shoulders. 'Spill.'

'I will explain.' His voice was still infuriatingly calm.

'Go on.'

'Not right now.' The mirror on the opposite wall lit up and Ren's face blinked into being. 'You need to shower, dress and

get some food.'

'Then you're going to have to come here with that food or I'm not going anywhere.'

She jumped off the bed and gasped as pain shot through her legs. She glanced down at her torn and muddy school uniform and though the bloody gash to her leg had gone, the pain still radiated across her skin. Her feet sank into deep carpet as she limped across the floor to the mirror. 'What the hell is going on?'

The screen went dark and text scrawled across its surface:

Date: June 21st 2375

Time: 12:15

Appointments scheduled: Lunch, 13:15 in Refectory, located level 231.

Her mouth dropped open at that last titbit. She had never been cleared above level one hundred and fifty-seven before. Stepping away from the mirror, she gingerly approached the window and gazed out. The rest of the city lay below her, the other towers finished at the hundredth and sixtieth floor. The building she was in towered above the rest of the city, and she froze as her head swum at the height. She was in the Capital Building, the tallest structure in the city.

Fighting back the urge to be sick, she backed away from the window and returned to the screen. The message was still bright against the surface, and she dismissed the reminder with a wave.

'Take a shower and get dressed,' Ren's voice echoed across the room and she turned to the door.

'You do not get to tell me what to do.' Despite the pain in her legs, she stormed across the floor to face him.

'I believe your military transfer order gives me that right.'

'Not when you're sending untrained civilians to the ground.' Her voice bounced off the walls and she saw him wince. 'So why don't you tell me what this is all about?'

'I promise I will tell what you need to know.' He held up a hand to stop her next outburst. 'But you need to get clean and eat something.' His voice softened. 'Please.'

It was the please that made her pause. 'Fine, I'll get ready. Then will you tell me what's going on?'

'I will,' he assured as he turned back to the door. 'Your belongings have already been brought here from your aunt's.'

'Is she …?'

'She's fine and aware of your situation.' His hand waved across the sensor and the door opened. 'The instructions are on your screen. I'll see you in the refectory.'

The door closed behind him and left Rosa alone. A wave of homesickness flowed through her as she stared out across the roofs of the city beneath her. Her old bedroom had faced one of the many rooftop parks that sprawled across the city and she missed the comforting sight of greenery. Outside of these windows, the sky seemed endless and the seeming isolation from the rest of the city made her feel lost. After a moment she opened the door to the closet and picked up some fresh clothing before heading for the bathroom.

* * *

Level two hundred and thirty-one was a floor below her, and she was not surprised to note that the elevator only serviced the top ten floors. Selecting the refectory, she was carried swiftly to her destination. The doors opened out onto a long corridor. The standard escape zones were clearly marked, and she felt herself begin to relax at the more familiar sight. A set of double doors led to the refectory and she approached them with caution, unsure of what to expect beyond.

The refectory was large and airy with many tables yet only one was occupied. To her annoyance, Ren was not one of the occupants. Instead two boys and a girl of about her own age sat there, an array of nearly empty plates and bowls before them.

'Hey, newbie.' The girl noticed her hesitant entry and beckoned her over. Beneath thick braids of emerald green hair, dark brown eyes sparkled in welcome. The other two said nothing but watched her with a quiet interest that she found unnerving. 'Don't be nervous, come on.'

Self-conscious and very aware of the array of empty tables around her, Rosa made her way across the floor.

'I didn't think Ren would find anyone,' one of the boys noted as she took the last place at the table. 'The last six recruits have been a complete bust.'

'Well, what do you expect?' The other boy noted, picking up his fork and spearing the last piece of pie on his plate. 'Not every potential succeeds.' He favoured Rosa with a long, speculative glance. He still wore the neural interface that identified him as a technician and she wondered what had brought him to this place.

'So, what's your thing?' he asked, ignoring her curious glance and leaned forward with an eager gleam to his eyes.

'Noah,' the girl said reprovingly. 'They've only just brought her in. She won't have gone through briefing yet.' Turning back to face Rosa, she continued. 'I'm Della, and that's Noah and Blake.'

'Rosa,' she replied, offering a tremulous smile. 'I don't understand what's going on.'

'Nor should you.'

Rosa jumped as Ren's voice sounded from the air around them.

'You haven't been briefed.'

A holographic projection rose from the middle of the table, and looked at the small group. 'Noah, I'd appreciate holding off on the questions until I've had a chance to explain the situation to our new friend.'

'Fine.' Noah gave a lazy wave. 'It'll be a boring conversation though.'

'But I want to know.' Rosa recovered from her bout of shock, and stared at the projection with some considerable anger. 'And you promised that you would tell me when I came downstairs.'

'I said you had to eat.' There was a definite snap to his voice. 'So that means eat.' The holograph clicked off and the others turned to face her.

'Wow,' Della replied. 'What did they do to you?'

'Dropped me in the middle of the pollution zone,' Rosa replied. 'And nearly got me killed.' Her fingers danced across the keypad on the table as she ordered carbonara.

'That's the standard orientation,' Noah replied with a yawn. 'Certainly nothing to get whipped up about.'

'Really?' Blake chuckled. 'You were so scared, they kept you in Iso for three days.' Noah coloured and threw a chip across the table. 'Not like Del here,' Noah nodded at the other girl. 'Three hours max.' He took a long sip of his drink. 'You didn't do too badly,' he pointed at Rosa. 'Two hours from arrival.

Guess you've got the gift ...'

'What gift?' she asked.

The trio exchanged a glance and went silent.

'No, really, come on,' Rosa urged as a chime sounded, signalling the arrival of her food.

'I don't know if we should,' Noah whispered as he leaned over the table. 'Ren said not to.'

'Oh, come on.' A bite of her food and she realised that she was ravenous.

'You'd better order another course,' Della noted as she typed another code into the app. 'You'll go through the calories like water.'

Rosa swallowed down another forkful of food, surprised at her level of appetite; she had never been this hungry before. Another chime and a tall glass of squash appeared by her elbow. The rest of the group returned to chatting about normal, inconsequential things as she cleared her plate.

'Better?' She looked up as Ren's voice echoed across the room. Rosa pushed aside her plate and glass and stood. 'Come on then,' he said, nodding towards the door. 'Let's take a walk.'

Rosa was very aware of the gaze of the others behind her as Ren fell into step beside her. In silence, they walked out of the refectory and into the wide corridor beyond.

Once free of scrutiny, Rosa rounded on him. 'What is going on? You nearly get me killed, and then you lock me in a dark room.' Ren winced slightly at her tone but said nothing. 'It's clear you have everything under surveillance, so why am I here?'

'One in ten thousand individuals test positive for a genetic abnormality at birth,' he began, the words making little sense to her ears. 'The abnormality is not always enough to warrant the transfer.' He stepped to the window at the end of the corridor and stared briefly out across the city. 'But it is monitored. Certain markers and traits will raise your profile, and after the usual school monitoring, the strength of the abnormality will determine whether the subject is given this transfer order.'

'But why did you have to ...?'

'The abnormality alone does not determine manifestation,' he explained. 'Extreme stress situations do.'

'What are you saying?'

'You've manifested class two electrical charge and increased strength.'

'You could have got me killed,' Rosa continued, the rage igniting the strange, sparkling energy that roiled within her.

'It would not have gone that far,' Ren continued, his eyes fixed on hers. 'If your abilities had remained dormant, then you would have been retrieved and re-processed.'

'Now what?' The anger stilled and grew quiet. A strange numbness caressed her senses as his eyes fixed on hers.

'Now you train.'

'For what?'

A grim smile lit his lips, but he did not answer. A bell tone chimed in the distance, and he glanced up. 'Get some more food, and meet us on level two hundred and thirty in twenty minutes.'

'But can't you just ...' Her voice trailed off as he walked away.

'Better get some more food.' She turned at the sound of Della's voice. 'You'll need the energy.'

Speechless, she watched the trio walk along the corridor

and enter the elevator. Left alone, she slowly re-entered the refectory and walked back to the table. Along one wall, tall windows offered a clear view to a clouded sky. The empty room was almost oppressive in its silence, and she sat, more to calm her nerves than anything else. Her stomach rumbled and she wondered once more at her increased appetite. Whatever she had done earlier that day had torn through her energy reserves leaving her with a hunger that needed twice her normal amount of food. Her fingers danced across the pad as she ordered quickly.

As she waited for the food to arrive, she thought back to the conversation in the hallway. The testing everyone did was expected, it ensured that people entered the needed professions as well as ensuring that the best candidates weren't wasted. But this transfer order was unknown to her. Her eyes flickered back to the window and she thought of her new billet. Ordinarily, she wouldn't have the clearance to even cross the skybridge to this building, and now she lived here. It was a shame she didn't wish to.

* * *

Twenty minutes later, she stepped out of the elevator and joined the small group of people in the corridor.

'Glad you made it.' Noah sounded sincere, and he was the only one who spoke. The others stayed silent and just nodded in her direction.

'Let's go,' said Ren as he walked out of a nearby door and led the group forward. 'Today, we'll be working on control and focusing.' He cast a quick glance at Rosa. 'As we have a new player, we'll need to slow up ...'

'Aren't you going to tell me anything?' Rosa interrupted, finally fed up with the cryptic nonsense.

'Very well.' Ren ushered the rest of the class forward. 'We're training you to defeat those creatures on level one.'

Stunned by the casual note to his voice, Rosa said nothing as he continued. 'Conventional small arms does little to them, and larger ordinances can destabilise the buildings.' He gave a small shrug. 'Welcome to the super-powered special forces.'

INTO THE WOODS

I packed the basket carefully. Bread, ham, some apples, cheese wrapped in cloth and small pot of butter. As mother bustled about the small hallway, I lifted my favourite red cape from the peg by the door.

'Now remember,' Mother placed a handful of silver into my pocket, money for the toll bridge, and slipped a slender knife into the scabbard on my belt. 'Use Heston's name if the toll keeper gives you grief and don't take the shortcut through the Spinney.' I barely listened to the instructions that she doled out every Sunday. This walk through the woods to Grandmother's house had been the same for the past two years and so were the instructions. None of Mother's dire predictions had come to pass in all of that time. The toll keeper accepted the money with a smile and, as for the Spinney? Well, it wasn't the dark pit of danger that Mother seemed to think it was. I fastened the heavy red wool cloak with a sigh and pulled up the hood.

'I'll be careful.' The words seemed to mollify her and she gave me a quick hug. The scent of beeswax and vanilla drifted across my nostrils before I pulled away and lifted the latch. 'See you tonight.'

Beyond the cottage door, the trees were laden with leaves of soft gold and red. The Autumn colours lifted my spirits as I traipsed through the crisp, bright morning. The trip to Grandmother's house was beautiful at this time of year, not too hot and not too cold and I smiled as I wove my way along the familiar path.

* * *

As expected, the toll keeper gave me no trouble and I crossed the bridge with a skip in my step. The rushing waters of the river barely captured my interest and I headed onwards with the heavy basket, eager to be free of its weight. Once past the river the road forked and, with barely a pang of conscience, I turned to the left-hand path that dipped towards the Spinney and the shortcut it offered. Despite Mother's worries as to the safety of the route, the Spinney was actually a quiet, hidden path through the very heart of the wood. Most people knew of it but few travelled it. Superstitions regarding fairies and monsters proved an effective deterrent to travellers. I crossed the last few steps and passed the boundary line. The Spinney was full with thick, closely-packed trees which blocked out the light. It was dim and cool beneath the boughs and, as always, I was struck by the sense of stillness that permeated the air. Stepping over a fallen log, I continued along the path. I was used to the strange silence that hung between the trees.

It wasn't fear that prickled my skin but the sensation of old magic, barely stirring in the dim light. It wouldn't harm me but I hurried anyway, eager to be free of the oppressive calm.

Another few paces and a cry echoed through the trees, stopping me in my tracks. The lingering scream faded and once more silence settled over me. It was a quiet tinged with foreboding, a hush that I felt at the base of my neck and deep in my stomach. Carefully, I took another few steps before the sound came again and soon after came the noise of running footsteps. Panicked, I dived to the side, hiding myself beneath the scrubby bushes beside the path. My blood pulsed frantically beneath my skin as my heart beat faster. Nervous tremors thrilled across my flesh and I hugged my arms around myself as I tried hard to remain still. I took several shallow breaths as I tried to calm down but it didn't work. All of my mother's tales and warnings rushed through my mind in an instant. *Stay out of the Spinney, stay on the road and stay safe.* A glance at the bright red of my clothing underscored the futility of hiding but I still hunkered down, hoping that the running figure would miss me.

He pounded down the path, desperation and terror vivid in his pumping arms and reddened features. Dark-haired, pale skin flushed red and blood running across his skin. He didn't glance in my direction as he raced past and a small sigh of relief hissed its way from between my lips. It was clear that he was running for his life. I held myself beneath the leaves, waiting for his pursuers to run past me. Yet none came. Instead, a loud yell and heavy thud sounded from along the path to my right and I knew that he had tripped over the log just a little further up.

I froze, lost in my indecision. Should I stay here and wait for whoever chased him to catch up? If they did, I would have to listen to the inevitable violence and, once they had finished with him, would I be next?

I wavered, torn between remaining in the dubious sanctuary of this bush and making sure that the boy got away. Moments passed and there was still no sound of pursuit and around me the Spinney returned to its usual calm. Carefully, cautiously I left my hiding place and moved out onto the path. The forest was clear, save for the crumpled form beside the log. With the sound of blood pumping in my ears, I headed along the path towards the young man.

'Help me.'

His pleading voice reached my ears as I drew closer. I could see the blood from the torn skin of his leg splattered against the dusty path like red petals.

'Please ...'

His face lifted from the bundle of leaves and bright blue eyes fixed on mine. Gingerly, I walked forward with every sense fixed on the other sounds of the forest.

'Please.'

I reached his side and held out a hand. The coppery scent of blood and musk hit me as my fingers curled about his and pulled him upright. 'Here.' I stopped as my eyes drifted across the bruises that were more clearly visible and I bit my lip. Whoever did this could be running down the path to finish him off at any moment. Silence still hovered about the trees and I held out my arm.

'Thanks.' His voice was hoarse and breathless. 'You shouldn't help me.'

'I'll just help you to the path.' He was right. I shouldn't help him but I didn't think I could turn away either. 'Just try to keep up.'

* * *

We walked in silence to the next fork in the road, the woods still deathly silent. He didn't speak but kept his head down watching the uneven path as his unsteady feet navigated each loose stone and pebble.

'Take that road," I said, pointing. 'There are caves to hide.'

'Thank you.' He pulled his hand free and began to move off. 'I'd leave the Spinney if I were you.' He called back over his shoulder. 'They're stopping everyone on the road.'

'What for?'

'Wolves as men,' he answered tersely. 'They'd do more than beat you.' He added as an afterthought. 'Go back to the main road.' He then turned his back and trudged off along the path, leaving me in the still forest.

I watched for a few moments more and then backtracked along the path and towards the main road. After this encounter, I was eager to be free from the Spinney. I reached the main crossroads and took the fork towards the village; Grandmother's house was just on the outskirts. As I passed the windmill, I could see a small group of people further along the road, gathered on the edge of the entrance to the Spinney. Each held a weapon of some sort and I gave them a wide berth.

'You, girl.' An older man hailed me as I drew close.

'Yes?'

'Have you seen the beast?'

'The beast?' I tripped over the words, wondering if he

meant the boy on the road.

'Yes, the wolf that walks as a man.' He advanced on me with short, fast steps and I tried to stay still as he reached my side.

'No.' I replied, thoughts running back to the time spent in the Spinney and the unusual, foreboding silence. Had the beast been roaming the woods? I shuddered at the thought and once more my mind ran back to the beaten boy on the forest path. Had he been the beast disguised as a boy? My heartrate sped up as I contemplated how close I had been to death.

'Of course she hasn't seen him, Father.' One of the other men called out. 'She would have been killed else, a pretty thing like that.'

Another breath to calm the beating of my heart. 'May I go?' I held up the basket. 'I'm delivering to my grandmother and she'll worry if I'm late.'

The elder man waved me past with a careless flick of his fingers and I returned to the path, being careful to walk sedately until I was out of their sight. As soon as the thick brush concealed me from their sight, I started to run, painful shocks running up my legs as my feet pounded along the path towards the relative safety of Grandmother's house.

* * *

Grandmother's house stood in a small clearing behind a low, neat wall that kept animals from trampling over her neat, well-tended garden. I reached the gate and passed through, heading for the door with faster steps than usual. My breath still came in panting gasps, evidence of my mad run through the forest. As I pushed open the door the scent of freshly-picked lavender drifted across, calming me as it always did. I dropped the basket to the floor and took a shuddering gulp of the scented air. My heart was still beating in triple time as I removed my glaring red hood.

"Red, dear is that you?"

I took another breath and plastered a fake smile onto my features as I picked up the basket and moved towards the kitchen at the back of the house. Grandmother was filling the kettle as I walked in and placed the basket on the table.

'Morning, Granny.' I reached up and gently kissed her cheek.

'What's wrong?' Grandmother's sharp eyes took in my flushed skin and still-rapid breathing. 'You've been running.'

'There's a patrol on the village road …'

'Ahh.' Grandmother held up her hand as she immediately grasped the significance. 'So Old Jonas hasn't found him yet?' She reached for the kettle and placed it on the fire.

'No.'

'Well, he wouldn't.' She sneered as she reached up to take two cups from their hooks. 'No sense or idea, that one.' She gave a snort. 'Has he found a convenient patsy yet?' My pulse quickened as I remembered the boy I had seen on the road. 'He's sure to serve up the nearest available scapegoat.' She thumped the teapot down onto the table. 'Which reminds me …' She stared straight at me. 'You're to stay here tonight. I don't want Jonas and his boozed-up goons deciding that you're fair game.'

'Yes, Granny.' I agreed, as she bustled about making the tea. 'What about Mother? She'll worry.'

'I'll send you straight home tomorrow. Now, let's have a

look at what you've brought me.'

I handed over the basket and watched as she placed the ham and cheese into the cold store. 'I saw a boy on the road,' I volunteered as she served us up two strong cups of tea.

'Not unexpected,' she muttered against the china as she took a swallow of the tea. 'Was he a member of Jonas's ruffians?'

'No.' I hadn't meant for my voice to come out so sharp. How could she think I would take note of those brigands?

'Well. If he has any sense, he'll find shelter.' She took another long drink and rested back against the chair. 'There's a beast out on the loose.' Her fingers drummed against the table and I stared at the heavy ring that always adorned her left hand. 'And Jonas is eager to bag another notch on his belt.' A rich, mocking chuckle echoed across the room. 'Bloody fool.'

I didn't say anything but just cradled the warm cup in my hands. My grandmother had always been sharper than my mother gave her credit for. But she never seemed to be concerned about the goings on in the forest beyond warning me to stay on the path.

'Still,' Grandmother shuffled back to the larder and cut a piece of cheese. 'It'll stir things up.'

'Yes, Granny.' I answered as I stared down at the dark liquid in the mug. Images of the terrified boy flashed through my mind and I sighed.

'Don't think about it.' Grandmother's wrinkled hand rested on my wrist. 'If he escaped during the day then …' She gave an airy wave. 'He'll be safe.'

'And if he doesn't?'

'Then he may be dead.' She ignored my look of shock as she picked up her cup and took it to the sink. 'And that'll be the end of it.'

'But you said he was a scapegoat ...' A niggling sensation of anger began to twist beneath my skin. It didn't seem fair or just to let an innocent youth die at the hands of Jonas and his mob.

'That he may be, but it's the last night of the moon and either way the beast will not be seen after tonight.' She dropped the cup onto the sideboard with a clunk. 'But if you intervene, then there'll be more death.' Her eyes fixed on mine. 'You understand? You must stay in and ignore whatever you hear.'

I watched her leave the kitchen with a heavy feeling in my chest. That poor boy had done nothing to earn the fate that Jonas and his crew would deliver and yet my grandmother would have me ignore it. Pouring the full cup of tea back down the sink, I walked from the kitchen towards the spare bedroom with my mind in turmoil. How could I stay aloof from whatever would happen this evening?

* * *

The moon had not yet risen but the night was clear and stars dotted the velvety sky as I struggled to find sleep. Through the window, I could see the ruddy glow of large fires from the village and I knew that Jonas had organised a fest to celebrate the capture of the beast or at least the death of one they could claim as the beast. My thoughts roiled within me as I tried to find a comfortable space in the bed.

With a sigh, I pushed aside the bedcovers and headed for the window. I rested my head on my hands and pressed my nose against the cold glass. The clear sky, the deep darkness of the woods and the orange glow from the village were arrayed before me. It could almost be beautiful were it not for the darkness that shrouded my thoughts.

A shadow raced across the woods and I stared. It was the young man, running beneath the starred sky and looking as terrified as he had done earlier. I glanced over my shoulder but all I could hear was the snoring of my grandmother from her room. A reckless, wild idea began to form in my mind and I pulled open the window.

'Come in here and hide,' I called, watching as the boy screeched to a halt at the sound of my voice. A look of relief crossed his features and he dashed to the window. I helped him inside and pushed him under the bed before closing the window and curtains. It seemed like only moments before the noise of the pursuing mob rushed by in a mess of whoops and jeers.

'Thanks.' The boy spoke with a trembling tone and I gave a smile as he pushed himself out from under the bed. 'You saved my life …'

'Red?' Grandmother's tremulous voice called from her room. 'What is it?'

'Nothing, Granny.' I tried to sound nonchalant but she left her room anyway. The boy made to dive beneath the bed as she flung open the door to my room.

'Oh, Red.' A look of frozen horror creased her features. 'You saved the boy.'

'Why is that so bad?' I argued as I pulled him to his feet. 'He doesn't deserve to die.'

'But do you?' A silvery light trickled through the thin curtains and brought a strange glow to the room. 'He needs to go outside now.'

'But …' I stopped as a strange prickling sensation began to run across my skin.

'Get him out now, girl, or you will regret it.'

I glanced at the boy and was stunned at the look of shock that covered his face, shock that was rapidly turning to terrified revulsion.

'You …' His voice was broken and cracked with fear. 'You're the beast.'

* * *

There was blood beneath my hands, on my tongue, in my hair, the scent filling my nostrils. I woke to the smell of the charnel house and the shredded remains of a boy I had wanted to save. I looked at my grandmother unable to ask or understand and she shook her head.

'You were safe alone and safe with me,' she explained as she drew me from the bloodied corpse. 'You would not have turned alone.'

'But Mother?'

'She knows, Red,' Grandmother sighed. 'That's why she worries so, why she sends you to me each week and for every full moon. For the beast skips a generation and your mother is safe, human. But you and I are …' She looked down at her hands. 'The moon alone does not cause the change or the insatiable hunger.' She pointed at the ragged gobbets of flesh and I gagged at the taste on my tongue. 'The presence of a victim does or a need to eat.' She stepped back from the door and sagged against the wall. 'I killed Jonas' flock in hunger the first night.' She rolled her eyes. 'Your reason leaves when you become animal. But I knew that the strange boy had arrived in the village …'

'And you served him up.'

'Of course. We always have.' Her grandmother wiped some of the blood from her cheek. 'It means that when the moon sets on the last day, the beast is seen to die. It keeps us safe and most full moons we do not need to kill. We just turn and sleep before the fire.' She chuckled. 'Damn shame tonight was a Blood moon and even more of a shame that you stayed awake.' She nodded to the empty cup. 'Normally the tea sends you to sleep and you never notice.'

'I've changed before?' My head was swimming with the revelation and I wanted to run and hide away from the knowledge that she was imparting. But I couldn't, not with the shredded corpse behind me and the taste of his flesh on my tongue. I wanted to gag again but I was beyond even that.

'Yes. Did you not realise that every full moon you stayed here, where I could watch you?'

'I hadn't …' And yet, thinking back, I had. I had spent every full moon with Grandmother and always with a different reason and each night I had slept like the dead, with no memory of the passage of time. 'And now what?' I couldn't think any further, the numbness seeping into my thoughts like cold treacle.

'Well, now you dig a hole and bury him.' Grandmother's voice was sharp as she pointed towards the corpse. 'And then we have to leave before Old Jonas starts hunting.'

HAVEN

'Sirius …' The thrum of the shuttle vibrated through the deck plates and Mai closed her eyes, visualising the sleek ship departing the bay. 'A Virago colony vessel, two hundred and fifty passengers and thirty crew destined for Gaia in the Sirius cluster.' She rattled off the statistics in a hushed, eager tone, as if speaking the ship's destination would bring her closer to it.

Mai had spent the last six years in the cramped and filthy confines of Haven, the transfer station that was the last stop for interstellar colony ships leaving the solar system. Beyond the reinforced, triple hull lay the blackness of space and the giant blue bulk of Neptune. The noise of departing ships had kept her company for most of that time, the promise of a new life keeping her from going crazy.

'Mai.' Her eyes blinked open as Harry interrupted her thoughts. 'You have a run.'

Mai dragged herself upright and stared at the man before her. Harry Lim was in his late sixties, stocky with grey hair and kind eyes framed by a pair of old-fashioned glasses. He had taken her in after her parents had died, giving her food and lodging in exchange for work. He was acid-tongued and occasionally grumpy, but kindness lay deep within him and he kept her safe.

'Where to?' Mai pushed a strand of dark hair out of her eyes and focused on the slim document in his hand. Mai was a runner, a courier for all those messages that could not be entrusted to internal communicators or for those that didn't merit the transmission fee. Bandwidth was at a premium on Haven and very costly. The slim envelope could hold anything, a trusted family recipe, orders from the local mart or, she took a breath, something illegal. It usually wasn't illegal, as Harry didn't like to involve his runners in shady dealings. But there had been the odd blunder and things had slipped through.

'Paradise Court.' An apologetic look creased Harry's face as he stated the destination. Mai rolled her eyes; Paradise Court was anything but. In a station full of low-lives and the destitute, Paradise Court was the worst. 'You're getting danger money,' he confirmed quickly as Mai's mouth dropped open. 'Here.' He held out the paper and Mai took it, hoping that the extra would cover the risk. The chip in her fingers activated and reacted with the ink. Dark streaks flowed from the document and slid into the skin on her hands. For a moment it trailed briefly across her palm the words flowing like black veins before settling into the familiar pattern of a diamond. As the last word faded from the paper Mai handed it back and reached for the red hoodie that lay across the back of a chair.

'You good?' Harry squeezed her upper shoulder and gave her a rare smile.

'I can handle it.' Mai shrugged on the hoodie and zipped it up. Harry's occasional forays into sympathetic encouragement always made her feel strangely sad.

'You're a good girl, Mai,' Harry reached into a cupboard and handed over a nutrition bar. 'Quick and conscientious, not as much trouble as the other louts.' As Mai's fingers closed on the bar, he pressed a credit chip into her palm. Her skin traced the credits and she raised an eyebrow at the amount. 'Call if you have trouble.' Another card entered her hand and she glanced at Harry in silent question. 'Paradise Court can be dangerous,' he stated by way of explanation.

'Thanks, Harry.' Mai pulled the red hood over her black hair, pushed the credit chip and token into her pocket and walked out of the small shop, trying not to cry. Harry could never be called her father, but he was the closest thing she had to one.

* * *

Moving out into the thoroughfare, Mai's senses were assaulted by the sights and sounds of the market. Haven's crowds swarmed across the space, filling the air with the sound of different languages and dialects. Most were from Earth, remnants of the world they had left behind and others were newly-created by those who remained and lived in that enclosed space.

Taking a left, Mai ducked into the warren of tunnels and service ducts that ran the length and breadth of the station. These shortcuts were small and crammed with rubbish that attracted the rats and cockroaches which had stowed away in supplies from Earth, but they were also the fastest way to traverse the two-mile long tin-can. They also attracted less savoury characters and Mai hoped that she wouldn't encounter any of them on her trip today. The hum of conversation from the market dulled as she raced through the cramped underbelly of the station, leaving her with the thrum of machinery and hiss of air from the ducts that lined the route.

Her feet pounded on the battered metal floor as she made the left turn onto Beggar's Run. The squalid corridor was packed at this hour and she had to slow down in order to pick her way through the crowd. This small part of the station was home to one of the many makeshift markets that serviced the poor district and the scent of spices and food mingled with the miasma of old sweat and worse.

"GET OUT OF THE WAY!"

Something solid smashed into her side and she hit the ground hard. Pain flared as her elbow slammed into the metal deck plate and she swore. The man who had knocked her over shouted an apology but did not slow his headlong flight. Following him in a whooping mass of sweat and muscle were a gang, ten-strong and laden with weaponry. Unable to regain her feet, Mai hunkered down and balled herself into a foetal position. Pounding feet smashed into the ground past her head and she prayed that none of them would land on her.

'That way ...'

Screams sounded as the gang tore through the lower market place, followed by the crash of falling stands. Mai picked herself up, the insults dying on her lips at the sight of the Century Ten gang motif emblazoned across the back of

their jackets. Of all the gangs that ravaged Haven's slums, they were the worst.

'You okay, Mai?' Anna shuffled over from her stall and helped her to her feet. Anna was in her forties but a harsh life made her appear older. 'Savages, the lot of them,' she snarled as she checked Mai for bruises. 'You steer clear of them.

'Yes, Mum.' Mai ducked the playful swipe the other woman aimed at her. 'Pretty dumb of that guy getting in their way.'

'Yeah?' Anna held out a small, gnarled apple. 'Well, you'd better make sure that you don't find yourself in their path. What's old Harry Lim got you running this route for, anyway?'

'I'm getting extra.' Mai didn't try to defend Harry to the other woman. Anna's protective streak could be over-powering and she didn't want to spend that much time here.

'Extra pay don't fix dead or worse,' Anna reprimanded as she readjusted Mai's hood. 'You be careful and don't let that old coot send you anywhere too risky.'

'Yes, Anna.' A soft smile drifted across the older woman's lips at her words. 'I'm going to take the eastern hub route.'

'Good thinking, as they were heading west.' Anna slipped her a small handful of dried blueberries and patted her shoulder. 'You'd better get running.'

'Thanks, Anna.' Mai started moving again and soon she was back in the white noise of the Warren, her feet moving almost soundlessly against the deck plates. In these moments she felt calm, almost at peace. The quiet murmuring of a fan blew slightly warm air across her legs as she ran, free for the moment of all cares with only the sensation of her legs moving in rhythm to her heart. In this whispering calm she allowed herself to think of her parents, dead these many years, and of her faint memories of their home on Earth. She had grown up in the crowded halls of Haven but she had not been born here. Alongside memories of cramped, filthy halls, visions of another life occasionally flickered into being. Images of a far-distant sky, vast skyscrapers and fat droplets of rain in air that wasn't recycled. Earth was crowded, almost full. The patches of country left were farms or desert. Vast cities criss-crossed the world and as such a steady stream of emigrants left to find fortune in some new world.

She bobbed through the eastern conduit and picked up the pace, feeling strands of her loose dark hair gently whisk across her face as she moved along the graffitied corridors with the elusiveness of mist. As she ducked into smaller spaces, thoughts of her mother drifted across her mind. What would she have thought of her daughter running the halls of Haven? Mai had to admit that she didn't know what her mother would have thought of her job as a courier. In these moments she liked to think that they had made their shuttle and reached the open space of the colonies. Virgin, unspoiled planets that humanity used for a new start. As she ducked along the next corridor she began to daydream of grass beneath her feet and fresh, unfiltered air. While Haven did have a park of sorts, it wasn't anything like the reality of Earth. Another right turn and Paradise Towers lay before her.

It was not so much a tower but a squat three-storey building. Graffiti scrawled across every surface and as she drew closer, her heart sank at the sight of the small group of thugs loitering before the main door. They noticed her and watched her approach. Briefly, she thought of trying later but that might provoke them to follow and she had a job to do.

Trying to feign nonchalance, Mai took a breath and walked towards the entrance.

'Fee.' The first boy moved to stand in her way, holding out a hand as he did so. 'No entry without.'

'Fine.' Mai stood her ground. 'Then you can explain to Campbell why his crew don't get messages.'

The boy was scarcely older than she and the colours he wore didn't link to any of the gangs in the district. He was a poser, a wannabe. Still dangerous, but hopefully open to intimidation by other, bigger fish.

'I'm sure they'll understand you taking a cut without permission,' she went on

'Fuck you, bitch.' The boy took a step forward and Mai had to control the fear that rippled down her spine. 'No one tells us what to do.' Was that a glint of steel in his belt? She didn't want to have to fight and with five of them she had little hope of succeeding.

'Don't be a twat, Jackser.' One of the other boys said and a flicker of hope seared into being. 'I recognise her. She's a courier and she knows Campbell. What if she tells him you're taking money without his permission?'

'How's he going to find out?' The boy snapped back. 'This bitch don't have the guts to tell on us.'

'Wanna bet?' Mai reached into a pocket and drew out the slender token that Harry had given her. 'Do you know what this is?' The small item was a gang pass. Even though Harry preferred not to deal with the gangs he'd made an exception for Campbell. Not that Mai had run any of those messages, but the card marked her as though she did.

'That's the Angel's sign.' The second boy backed up a step

followed by two of the others. 'You don't wanna mess with their couriers.'

Mai held firm and kept eye contact with Jackser who eventually stepped back, his desire to be the big man clearly warring with the sense to keep clear of Campbell and his crew.

'Fine.' He moved to one side and she stepped past him and into the building.

* * *

Paradise Tower always smelled like a mixture of boiled cabbage, strong disinfectant, urine and vomit. Another reason why Mai hated runs to its squalid, dim hallways. There were always malfunctions with the lighting and the security that was supposed to run the place was absent. From down the next corridor she could hear the sounds of an argument and she kept going. Arguments more often than not became violent here and the last thing she needed to be was collateral in a domestic dispute.

A snap of her fingers and the address flared into being on her hand. Heading for the stairs, she took them two at a time, hoping to finish the job quickly. The upper hallway was thick with the scent of weed and she hurried to the end of the corridor as she avoided the rubbish that lined the floor.

'What do you want?' Fatigue lines creased the woman's face as she pulled open the door. 'I'm not buying.'

'I'm not selling.' Mai held out her arm. 'Got a message.'

'Wait there.' The woman reached behind her and pulled a reader from a battered table. There was a buzz as she entered the retrieval code and held it out. The display blinked red and Mai pressed her thumb into the slot. Once again, the strange hum pulsed through her bones as the ink slid from her skin.

The door shut in her face without thanks and Mai headed back down the corridor, relief rippling through her veins. She moved back along the hall and headed out into the courtyard. Thankfully, the louts from earlier had moved away from their position by the door and she raced off towards the tunnels with a lighter heart.

* * *

The trip back was always faster than the trip out. Mai practically skipped through the warren of white noise, still alert for any signs of trouble. A blockage in tunnel three forced her to backtrack and she headed deeper into the bowels of Haven.

The lights were dimmer here and she felt her heart-rate increase slightly. Bad things happened in darkened corridors. She was heading towards the seventh intersection when a figure loomed out of the shadows before her. Startled she attempted to swerve but ended up skidding to the floor, her ankle twisting painfully as she did so.

'Are you hurt?' A strange husky voice issued from the man's lips as he stepped forward. 'I'm sorry … I …'

Mai glanced into the man's face and she backed off with a yelp. It wasn't the blood from a severe beating that made her move or even the physical presence of him. It was his eyes. They were shaped like a cat's and gold with vertical irises. Those eyes were the reason for the panic that rippled across her flesh. He wasn't a gang-banger or a dust-head, he was a splice – a genetic anomaly and much more dangerous than any human thug.

'Don't scream, please …'

Mai scuttled back on her heels but only succeeded in hitting the wall.

'I won't hurt you.'

'I bet that's what you all say.' Mai struggled to stand but her ankle wouldn't take her weight and she slumped down again. A hurt look crossed the man's face but he stopped moving. 'Just leave me alone,' she said.

'Here?' He waved a hand at the surrounding area. 'I wouldn't leave anyone here.' He took another breath. 'I promise you're safe with me.'

Mai looked at his outstretched hand and back into the dim light of the intersection. With her ankle in this state, she was a target for any of the tunnel scum that moved between levels. True, trusting a splice was not much better. However she had little choice.

'Okay.' She stretched out her hand and he helped her up.

'Where are you going?' His words were measured and careful as though he had to think about the meaning of each word.

'The Plaza, level two.'

Actually, Harry's place was a couple of halls away but she didn't want to bring a splice back to her home. She may need the assistance at this moment, but she wasn't stupid.

'Okay.'

He supported her as she began the long, hobbling and painful walk through the corridors of Haven. Not that she would have admitted it, but she was grateful for his help. Whatever damage she had done to her ankle would take days to heal.

'What happened to your face?, she asked after several moments of silence.

'Gang.'

Mai cast her mind back to the chase she had witnessed earlier.

'Century Ten?' Now another fear began to wriggle against her thoughts.

'Yes.'

'Are they still looking for you?'

'I hope not,' he replied. 'I didn't appreciate our first meeting.'

He led her along the upper corridors and through the first thoroughfare and, for once, Mai was grateful for the emptiness of the location. Should anyone see her with a splice …

'I'll try not to get you killed.'

Her head whipped round at his words. Could splices read minds?

'I may be a splice but I'm not a monster.'

'How do …'

'I read it.'

She cringed away from the vertical irises that were boring a hole into her face.

'It's all over you. Your fear.' There was a strange tenseness to his words that made her cringe. 'And I wish you weren't afraid.'

'Why?'

'Because I'm not a monster.' The anger in his voice caused her to look up in surprise. 'I never asked for this.'

'But I thought …' She couldn't continue with what she thought. All she knew of splices was the warren gossip. That they were criminals and former soldiers volunteering for a last gasp at redemption.

'I was an orphan on Pandora,' he said with a bite of anger. 'I was promised food and a bed if I went to the orphanage.' Mai almost came to a stop as the impact of his words hit her like a bolt. 'But it was a lie. I went to sleep and woke up,' he waved his hand over his body. 'Like this.'

Mai's mouth worked as she tried to find the words to respond. She had always known that orphans were vulnerable out here, always known that protectors like Harry were few and far between but this …

'I …'

'Don't apologise. It's nothing you did.' He helped her across the next pile of rubble and lapsed back into silence. They continued along the corridor in a tense silence. Thoughts chased themselves around Mai's head as she discarded conversation after conversation. What could she say that wouldn't seem trite?

'Were you born here?' he asked.

'No,' she replied with a small shake of her head. 'I was born on Earth.' She wasn't sure why she was volunteering this information to a stranger and a splice at that. 'My parents came here for transit to one of the colonies. They died when I was little.'

'I'm sorry.' Once more silence reigned as they picked their way along the corridor. 'Are you waiting to travel? he asked eventually.

'Don't have the money,' she answered. 'I'm stuck here. Harry pays well enough for the runs but I'll never get the money to leave.' After all, if Harry Lim had the money, he would have left the station years ago.

'What about going back to Earth?'

'There's nothing for me there, even if I could afford it.' She stopped speaking, aware that melancholy was beginning to take hold. Though Harry had taken care of her it wouldn't be forever and she had seen the remnants of those lost on Haven. She knew that this fate loomed large in her future. Once again, thoughts of the colony ship Virago raced through her mind. The colony ships meant salvation, a new life on another world if only she could afford the passage.

The splice opened his mouth only to close it again. There was very little he could say to her troubles and they were by no means unique.

'One more hall to go.' His voice dragged her from her thoughts and she stared at the winding corridor before her. Sounds of the market drifted towards them and relief rushed through her. They continued to move along the hallway only to stop suddenly as the splice froze in place. 'Ahh, shit.'

'What is it?'

'Someone's coming.' He pushed her back against the wall and directed her towards the small pile of rubbish. Mai dived into the collection of sacking as she heard the sound of footsteps racing along the hallway. As she covered her red hoodie with the filthy blankets, she saw the gang run into view.

'Hey. boys, here's the Gene Freak.' The leader catcalled as he walked forward. Behind him the other ten members of the gang edged closer with identical, anticipatory grins on their faces. Mai snuggled deeper into the blanket, hoping that they didn't look in her direction. 'I don't think he learned his lesson the first time.'

'And what lesson would you teach me?' His voice was

mocking. 'Dance steps? Fashion? How to win friends?' There was scuffle of feet as he ducked the clumsy swing. 'I doubt there's anything you could teach.'

Another one lunged forward only to slip and slam heavily into the ground. Mai held her breath as the thug pulled himself upright. There was the sound of fist meeting flesh as the leader finally landed a punch. Mai winced at the grunt of pain and briefly closed her eyes as the rest of the gang moved in.

'Hold him, boys.'

Mai opened her eyes again and peeked out of the blanket. The splice was pressed against the wall, blood running freely from his nose and lip. As she looked on in horror, she caught the slight shake of his head as he silently warned her to stay hidden. The gang moved closer and the punches began to fly.

Mai was no stranger to scenes of violence; it was after all a common occurrence in the lower warrens of the station. But that didn't mean she had seen it this close up before. The leader and his second took turns to punch and even kick the splice till his face was black and blue with bruises. Mai huddled deeper into the blanket with each blow and spray of blood.

Time lost all meaning as she cowered there, hoping that someone would interrupt the horrific scene before her.

'See, boys …?' There was a break in the torment as the gang leader pointed at the splice with a bruised and bloodied finger. 'Healing already.' His fist slammed into the splice's face. 'Can't do enough to beat 'em to death.' There was a metallic sound and he drew a dagger from his belt. 'But this …' There was a cry of pain as the blade sliced across a forearm. 'This will make it a lot faster.'

He nodded to two of his men. 'Hold his head up.' The

leader moved closer.

Terrified that she was going to be witness to a murder Mai finally pushed herself free from the blankets and screamed.

The leader spun round and his crew froze. Mai, afraid of the shark-like grins that spread across their faces, began to back away towards the coolant corridor.

'Come here, girly.'

The closest gang member lunged for her and she darted back out of reach her ankle screaming with pain as she did so. As he tried to grab her for the second time the splice used the distraction to bust free. Before Mai's startled eyes he lifted his head and with an animalistic growl he tore his arms free. As the leader rushed forward with another punch the splice dived to one side and, with a powerful wrench of his arms, snapped the man's neck in one swift move.

Mai's mouth fell open and she stopped moving, startled by his sudden and violent recovery. Her eyes fixed on his bruised features and was startled to see that the bruising did not appear to be as bad as before.

'Leave the girl alone.' He spoke, his voice ragged either from pain or anger. She couldn't tell which. 'I let you beat me. but …' He leapt at the man near Mai sending him sprawling to the floor. 'You don't touch the girl.'

Mai gave a small cry as she watched his fingers grow into claws. There was an anguished scream and blood sprayed along the corridor soaking into her trousers. The splice turned back to the men who had held him, hands dripping with arterial blood.

The remaining en took flight down the corridor and out of sight, leaving the two of them alone with the corpses and gore.

Mai stepped back. 'What did you do?' The claws shrunk back and he looked down at the bodies.

'We heal fast,' he muttered as he wiped his hands on the gang member's coat. 'If you hadn't come out …'

'They were going to kill you and then they would have found me,' Mai retorted, her eyes still fixed at the bodies on the floor.

'Girl …'

'It's Mai Li.' Her breath came in panicked gasps. 'And the authorities …' She reached forward and tugged at his arm. 'They'll come for you, they wouldn't have bothered that much if you hadn't killed them. But now …'

'The company will call for a search crew I know.' He sighed and pushed a hand through his hair. 'No good deed and all that.'

'You've got to get off the station.' She moved down the corridor and stopped when she saw the trail of bloody footprints. 'There's a colony ship leaving for Epsilon Indi in half an hour.' She ducked to the gang leader's pockets and pulled forth a selection of credit chips. 'Check him.' She pointed to the other gang member as she wiped her bloody shoes on the discarded blanket and wiped the obvious blood from the legs, thankful that she was wearing black leggings.

'There's five hundred here,' he said.

'Good and with the thousand here, that'll get you a berth on the colony ship.' She pressed the chips into his hand. 'Now go.'

The splice glanced down at the bodies and then back at her. 'What if they come for you?'

'I've got friends,' she answered, remembering Campbell's

token in her pocket. 'And besides, you took out Century Ten. They'll be too busy warring each other to worry about me.' She took another breath. 'Just go.'

'Thank you.' He held out a hand and she took it. Despite the blood that smeared her hand, his grip was gentle. 'I'm Lowell.' The distant sound of a siren echoed along the corridor and he released her hand to run off down the corridor and out of sight.

She waited until his footsteps had faded before she limped along the last corridor to the crowded market and Harry's home.

'You alright, Mai?' The old man's voice nearly brought her to tears as she nodded and walked past him towards the bathroom.

'I twisted my ankle,' she called back as she pulled the door closed behind her and removed her bloody clothing. 'But the run's finished.'

"Good girl."

She heard Harry bustle around the kitchen as she pressed a cold compress against her ankle. As the cold leeched the pain from her flesh, she removed the red hood and something fell to the ground from her pocket. Curious she picked up the small item and stared at the miniature figurine of a wolf. It couldn't be considered valuable but she understood and appreciated the small gift. As she limped into the shower she wondered if Lowell had made the colony ship and if she would ever see him again.

* * *

One year later.

'Come on, Mai. You've got a fast run to Haven Heights,' Harry called as she scoffed the last piece of toast. 'Make sure you've got clean shoes.'

Haven Heights was the most expensive residence – if there was such a thing – on the station and most of the station personnel had quarters there. As such, the fee for such runs were quite high and usually taken by bigger firms, so this run was very welcome. She reached Harry's side and held out her arm.

'It's a pickup,' he said as the address flowed into the chip. 'Should be a nice payday.'

'Great,' she replied as she pulled the familiar red hoodie from the peg. 'Contact?'

'Anjuli Chopra, head of communications.'

'Right.' Taking a last sip of tea, Mai headed out and back into the thoroughfare, wondering why the communications head was requesting such a low-grade courier for the transmission of messages. But she didn't worry for too long, money was money and what she would make on this run would bring her closer to a more comfortable existence.

* * *

In no time at all she reached the entry to Haven Heights. Unlike most of the station, Haven Heights had its own park and climate rooms and she could see people walking through different habitats, the greenery staving off the grey monotony of the station. Fighting back the familiar pangs of jealousy, she headed for the main entrance.

'Permission?' A robotic voice issued from the box on the

wall.

'Mai Li, courier for Lim's Messenger Service.' She held out her hand and her identity number bloomed across the palm. There was a small whirring noise followed by a bell tone and the door slid open. She entered the wide hallway and the instructions imbedded in her hand directed her to the lift at the end of the hall. White noise swirled about her as she was carried swiftly to the top floor. Real plants lined the walls and delicate scent of growing things lifted her spirits as she reached the door at the end of a hallway.

The door opened on her knock to reveal a tall, elegant woman clad in the drab uniform worn by the station personnel.

'Ms Chopra?' she asked and was rewarded with an affirmative nod. 'You needed a courier?'

'Not quite.'

Mai felt her heart sink as the woman stretched out a hand and handed her a small package.

'I don't deliver.' Runners like her didn't handle physical items and she cringed at the thought of losing the money for the run.

'You misunderstand, this isn't a delivery.' The communications officer interrupted her spiel and pressed a brown paper package into her palm. 'The captain of the Space Dancer asked me to ensure that this got to you.'

'Me?' She felt the weight of the packet and glanced up at the other woman. 'But I don't know any ...'

'The instructions were quite specific.' She picked up a small pad and read: 'To be handed to Mai Li, courier for Lim's Messenger Service.' As Mai stared at the package in her hand, Chopra waved her back towards the door. 'Now I'm off duty, so if you wouldn't mind?'

'Oh.' Mai nodded and stepped out of the apartment in a daze. She had never received anything from off-world before.

The sound of the door shutting behind her woke her from her daze and with some speed she left the complex and returned to Harry's.

* * *

A customer was keeping Harry busy as she crossed the threshold of the small office and headed for her room. Closing the door, she sank down on her narrow cot before finally looking at the package in her hand. It was wrapped in brown paper and had her name clearly printed on the outside. Taking a breath, she slid her finger beneath the tape and carefully pulled the wrapping free.

An envelope lay on top of a bubble-wrapped pair of items. Mai stared at the hidden shapes before she turned to the envelope and the letter that lay within.

Mai,

I know I don't know you well and that we didn't speak much, but I have to say how grateful I am that you helped a Splice when you didn't have to. I made my ship on time and am now waiting at the refuelling station near Barnard's Star before making the last jump to Epsilon. I've been lucky here on station. It's a place where Splices can make a living without too many worries, so I'm secure here, more than I was in the Sol System. It isn't an exaggeration to say that I would have died on Haven and I have you to thank for my survival. On the credit stick enclosed is a small amount of funds that'll help you make that leap to Epsilon, Sirius or Proxima, wherever you wish to go.

My thanks for all you did.

Lowell

PS. The passcode for the credit chip is the name of the group that bought me my freedom

Mai ripped open the bubble-wrap and watched as the credit stick and the small statuette of a wolf spilled out across her lap. She stared at the small figure for a moment before turning her attention to the credit stick. She pressed her thumb against the activation sensor and tapped the words *century 10* across the keys and waited. "Seven hundred." She breathed as the amount flickered across the readout. It wasn't a fortune but that colony ship berth was now no longer a fantasy. A smile inched across her face as she read the letter again before transferring the money to her account. Taking the statuette into her hands, she rested back against her tiny cot as the deck plates shuddered once more with the departure of yet another colony ship.

'Skylark.' She repeated her usual mantra with a sense of renewed hope. 'A Siren Class supply vessel destined for Epsilon Indi.'

WHISPER

There was a crack as the wooden bat smacked the small, white ball into the air and away from the hands struggling to catch it. Poppy watched the ball sail over her head with a sigh of resignation. She knew what would happen next.

'Fetch the ball!' Megan shouted from the other end of the pitch and Poppy nodded with only a small grumble as she strode from the freshly-cut lawns of the school playing field and into the wilder woods that lay beyond. As she trudged through piles of dead and decaying leaves, she wondered why they had decided to play rounders in late October. Misty air chilled her skin through her hoodie as she moved deeper into the woodland.

As she searched the ground, the noise from the games pitch seemed to fade behind her and she glanced back through stark, leafless trees and a mist that would put a Hammer

horror film to shame. Even though the pitch was close to her, she could barely see it, wreathed as she was in cold, white fog. The shouts of the others seemed muffled and far away. She swallowed nervously.

It seemed too quiet here beneath the skeletal trees and she began to hunt faster, strangely afraid of her foggy, chill surroundings. She scoured the ground for the ball, wondering how it seemed to have come so far into the trees. Emma Langley didn't hit *that* hard.

A branch snapped nearby and her head jerked up towards the sound, her heart thumping as she struggled to control the urge to run.

'Come on, Poppy!' Megan's voice jolted her into motion and she took another step forward only to scream as the ground fell away beneath her feet and she fell, her ankle snapping painfully beneath her as she skidded and tumbled into a deep pit. The ground rushed past as she fell, her fingers digging into the crumbly soil, fragile nails tearing as they failed to slow her descent. Twigs scored into the soft flesh of her legs, drawing blood as she tumbled headlong into darkness.

She came to a stop in a pit of soft, loamy earth fragrant with decay. The soft powdery soil cushioned her body and she slowly pushed herself upright, her ankle screaming with each movement.

'Pop?' Megan called and she glanced upward towards the distant exit. 'Are you okay?'

'I think I've broken my ankle,' she shouted back, grateful that her voice didn't shake. 'Get Mrs Lawton and the nurse.'

'Just hold on.' Bits of earth drifted down and settled into Poppy's hair as the other girl took off in a run, leaving her to shift uncomfortably within the tear in the earth.

Her ankle throbbed and any attempt to move made it hurt more, so Poppy resigned herself to this semi-prone position on a bed of compost and bugs. Stillness settled around her like a blanket as she waited in the soft darkness. From above she could still hear the excited chatter of her classmates. Oh, they were concerned but the excitement of her fall loomed larger than their worry.

As she tried not to think about the bugs infesting the loamy soil beneath her, Poppy began to focus on her surroundings. She had fallen into some burrow or cave. The shadows clustered around her were only partially dispelled by weak light from above and in the formless darkness a spike of fear jolted down her spine. What had made this hole and how deep was she beneath the ground? Something skittered across her hand and she jolted upright, nearly screaming with both fear and pain as she shook her hand, vigorously dislodging whatever creepy-crawly had made its way across her skin. .... 'Just calm down,' she whispered to herself as her heart thumped loudly within her chest. 'It wasn't going to eat you.' Her words sounded hollow as she tried not to move from the soft pile of earth beneath her.

A small shower of dirt dislodged from the hole above and she bit back a small cry. Images of being buried in this crumbling burrow began to fill her mind and she stifled the whimpers of fear that threatened to tip her into panic. One of the girls shouted something encouraging that she could not fully hear, too occupied with the pain, the fear and the shivering cold that had begun to infest her limbs.

'Come on ...' She pleaded at the light above her. 'Just hurry up.'

Grains of soil drifted against her skin and she bit her lip, praying that the edges of the hole would hold firm. Once more she heard the distant chatter from above and controlled the urge to swear at them. She was in pain, laying in a mixture of dead leaves, insects and what she hoped was mud and they were treating it as something exciting.

'She won't be long.' Megan's voice drifted down into the darkness. 'Are you okay?'

'Absolutely peachy,' Poppy muttered as she tried once more find a comfortable position. 'I'll have to visit next year for my holidays.'

'What was that?' Megan called back.

'Nothing …' Poppy called back. 'Absolutely nothing.'

Sarcasm helped keep some of the fear at bay but she felt the oppressive weight of the darkness around her. Her ankle continued to throb as quiet descended on the small hollow. Even the noise from above seemed to fade as she resigned herself to her situation.

In the stillness, her body seemed to slow down and relax. The strange shudders that ran across her skin began to subside and a warming lassitude seemed to seep through her flesh. Her head swam uncomfortably, so it seemed only natural to rest back against the soft earth and close her eyes.

'You don't want to do that.'

Her eyes snapped open at the voice that called from nearby. Her eyes flickered around the room wildly as they looked for the source of those words.

'It's dangerous.'

As her eyes adjusted once more to the dim light they

focused on the other side of the burrow and the man-shaped shadow that had not been there before.

'Who?' She stuttered out. 'How?'

'I'm a friend,' the shape whispered as it came closer.

Still unable to move, Poppy attempted to push herself backwards and away from the advancing figure, not at all mollified by his claims to friendliness.

'And you're going into shock.'

The figure reached the light and Poppy shied backwards at the furry, wolfish features that came close. A pair of bright blue, almost human eyes stared at her as the creature came to a stop just within touching distance.

'I …' Confusion raged through her mind as the figure came closer. 'Who are you and what are you doing?'

'Making sure shock doesn't kill you.' His voice was soft like liquid silk and she found herself drifting closer, almost drawn by the hypnotic cadence of his words. He reached out and made a firm mound of earth before carefully lifting her legs onto it. 'Do you still have circulation?'

'Yes.' Bewildered beyond thought, Poppy could only nod dumbly to his questions as he checked her for signs of bleeding. 'Who are you?'

'You have a cut on your temple. That'll need seeing to.' He dodged her question as he continued to check her for injuries.

'But …'

A voice came from above 'Poppy, are you alright?'

She glanced up as Mrs Lawton leaned over the edge of the pit.

'I'm fine … I …' Poppy turned back to the creature and stopped. Her helpful shadow was nowhere to be seen. 'Just hoping to get out.' She glanced around at the dark, shadowy burrow for signs of her saviour but there was nothing.

As Mrs Lawton and a couple of the gardeners made their way into the burrow, she kept looking for her blue-eyed saviour. Her feet were still propped up on the mound of earth yet there was no sign of the person who'd placed it there.

'We'll get you out of there in a moment." Mrs Lawton's voice interrupted her search and she lay back against the earth, wondering if she had dreamed the last few minutes.

* * *

By the middle of the next day, she was heartily sick of remaining in the infirmary. She had only sprained her ankle but the nurse had wanted to monitor her for shock. Not that she was complaining, for by now she had convinced herself that her visions in the hole were the results of trauma. In the bright, cold light of the infirmary, she had begun to question her experiences and it became even easier to dismiss them as stray visions brought on by a blow to the head. Half-wolf men were the realm of fairy tales and urban fantasy, restricted to the pages of pulpy paperbacks that several of her friends devoured by the dozen. No one believed that these things could exist in real life. At least, that's what she told herself, even though the memory of his voice still thrilled through her mind.

She shifted uncomfortably in the infirmary bed, her ankle protesting with every move she made. It hadn't taken them long to lift her out of the hole and back to the school. The nurse had loaded her with painkillers and she had soon fallen into a deep sleep, a sleep full of images of wolves with bright, overly-human, blue eyes.

In the distance, she heard the lesson bell and wondered what was happening in double maths as she lay here in the strange quiet of the infirmary. She drifted in and out of sleep, still too fuzzy-headed to remain awake. The nurse came and went and soon the infirmary darkened as night fell.

She woke with a start at the sound of movement. 'Who's there?' She pushed herself up on her pillow and glanced up at the dark shape on the other side of the room.

There was the sound of a cupboard closing as the figure straightened up at the sound of her voice.

'Nicholas.' The shape turned and Poppy's mouth dropped open as his rich, familiar tones filled the room. 'I didn't mean to wake you.'

'You.' She pulled herself upright and stared at the man. 'It was you.'

'It was me … what?'

She switched on her side light and stared at the young man in confusion. For a moment she had been back at the bottom of the pit, listening to silky words from an impossibility. The person before her wasn't that vision, his hair was a dirty blonde and tousled above a fairly ordinary face. One of the upper-sixth who populated the school and yet … that familiar voice had thrilled through her.

'I just thought …' She bit her lip and shrank back against the pillows feeling foolish for what she had imagined. 'Never mind. The nurse isn't here at the moment.'

'I can see that,' he replied with a slight smile. 'I'm sorry to wake you.' He turned back and began to walk towards the exit. 'Let the nurse know I came by.'

'Wait a minute.'

He turned towards her and her voice stuttered to a halt. In the lamplight she could see his eyes, impossibly blue and deep. 'I didn't catch your surname.'

'Lyall,' he called as he walked through the door. 'Hope you get better soon.'

As the door closed behind him, Poppy ran her mind back over the sound of that voice. Such a voice, almost hypnotic, a dream voice that she had consigned to the stuff of fantasy. She rolled over and buried her head in the pillow trying hard to dismiss the thoughts that had begun to flit through her head – thoughts of wolf-men in the dark.

As she tossed and turned, a shadow crossed the room, cast by the light of a full- moon. On unsteady feet, she pulled herself from the bed and towards the window. The infirmary overlooked the woods which were now wreathed in mist beneath the silvery light.

The windowsill was cold against her hip as she leaned against it, staring out at the moonlit, misty landscape in a fugue. The clouds swept from the sky, leaving the grounds bathed in silver. Beneath the soft light, the features of the school grounds were pale and ghostlike and as she surveyed the altered landscape, she froze in shock. A figure was loping across the lawns – a bent, misshapen figure that brought to mind visions of wolves as men.

Ignoring the sharp, blinding pain in her ankle she raced back to bed and burrowed deep beneath the covers trying hard to forget what she thought she had seen.

* * *

Sunlight streamed through the window and woke her from her fitful, haunted sleep. The nurse was back at her station and the strange apparitions of the night before seemed distant in the warm light of a new day.

'Let's have a look at your ankle, dear.' The nurse pulled back the covers and stared at the swollen flesh with concern. 'It's very swollen, can you move your toes?'

Poppy attempted to comply but the pain made her hiss and tears came to her eyes. Clearly, the ill-advised dash across the infirmary floor had done more damage. The nurse busied herself and pressed yet another cold compress to the ankle before handing over another couple of aspirin.

'I think another night here, just to be sure,' she said as she replaced the covers and headed back to her station. 'I'll have Mrs Lawton send up the work for your classes today.'

'Nurse Blake,' Poppy said, remembering her night-time encounter.

'Yes, dear?'

'A man was here last night, looking for you.'

'A man?' A confused look creased the nurse's features. 'What man?'

'He said his name was …' She struggled to remember; her memory fuzzy from sleep. 'Nicholas … something …Nicholas Lyall.'

The nurse didn't answer and yet a stricken look had creased her features. 'Are you sure he said he was Nicholas Lyall?'

'Yes.' Her throat contracted as a feeling of unease prickled across her skin. 'Very blue eyes, seemed to be a sixth former.'

'I doubt that,' the nurse said with forced joviality. 'You would have been dreaming. Perhaps you've seen his picture in the school hall?'

'No.' She wasn't sure of much, but she knew that he had been there. 'I saw him as clear as I saw you, he was taking something from the cupboard.'

'My dear, you've had a shock and that does odd things to the mind.' The nurse placed a comforting hand on her shoulder. 'I know you could not have seen Nicholas Lyall.'

'Why not?'

'Because he disappeared ten years ago.'

Poppy felt her stomach fall at the words.

'It was a tragedy.' The nurse brushed a tear away. 'He had such a bright future ahead of him.'

'What happened?' A cold feeling of dread raced up Poppy's spine. He had been before her as clear as day.

'You don't need to …'

'Please tell me?' She couldn't stop now, the strangeness of the last few days gnawed at her and she couldn't let this go.

'He was bitten by a dog and came to the infirmary for treatment.' A tear rolled down the older woman's face. 'The wound became infected and he grew delirious throughout the evening and when I went to call an ambulance, he vanished. We searched everywhere but there was no trace.' She brushed the tears from her cheeks. 'He didn't even take his clothes. There was a full investigation but nothing was discovered.' The nurse gave herself a shake. 'So, it couldn't have been him. You've probably seen his picture in the memorial hall, heard his story and imagined him in your fever." She handed over a glass of water. 'Now, take a drink and try to get some rest.'

As the nurse left the room, Poppy tried to settle back down in the bed and get some sleep. While the nurse's idea of shock had some merit, she knew she had never heard about Nicholas Lyall before last night. As she stared up at the ceiling, she decided that as soon as her ankle was better, she would head back into the woods and discover the truth.

* * *

It was a bright and cold November morning when Poppy crossed the lawns towards the trees. It had taken a month for the damage to her ankle to fully heal and even now she felt a slight twinge if she moved too quickly. She had intended to travel out to the woods before now, but school and her friends had made it difficult to leave on her own.

A slight crust of frost dappled the grass and leaves as she left the sports field behind and headed into the woods. Moving slowly and checking the ground, she headed deeper into the trees looking for … well, she wasn't sure. It took about ten minutes to find the hole she had fallen into and she stayed away from the edge, unwilling to risk another fall. It was quiet here and, despite the bright sunshine, a shiver that wasn't from the cold ran across her skin.

'This is stupid,' she spoke aloud as she came to a halt, the words an effort to dispel the nervous tension that creased her skin. 'There's no such thing as werewolves.'

'Are you so sure?'

She shrieked as the silken tones echoed across the clearing.

'Seems like you're trying hard to disprove it.' He walked out of the woods; his clothes strangely well-kept for someone who may have lived in the wilderness for years.

'Nicholas?' she asked and he nodded his head. 'They said you'd disappeared.'

'Well, they were right.' He stepped a little closer and stopped. 'I thought it was better than pretending to be normal and hiding once a month.'

'There's no such things as …'

'Then why are you looking for me?'

'To prove that you were a delusion,' she answered, her voice trembling from cold and stress. 'I didn't think you were real.'

'No, you knew.' He scuffed a toe into the ground. 'I can't blame curiosity.'

'Why has no one else …?'

'Seen me?' He reached down and picked up a handful of dirt. 'Well, I hide quite well and no one else has raced through the woods.'

'I didn't race.'

He gave a small smile and she continued, feeling some of the nervousness leave her. 'And while I thought I dreamed you, I really wanted to thank you for keeping me awake.'

'I may not want to be seen but I wouldn't leave someone hurt.' He sat down on a log and indicated another log nearby. Poppy sat and stared across at him. 'To be honest I wanted to be seen.'

'You did?'

'Of course.' He ran a hand through his hair. 'There's only so much loneliness I can take.'

'Do you hide in the school?' She remembered his night-time visit to the infirmary.

'Yes, they have many disused rooms at our school and it means I get to have a shower from time to time.' A rueful look creased his features. 'Living in the woods is not good for personal hygiene.'

'And why do you look the same age?'"

'Part of the gift of being a werewolf seems to be eternal youth. I guess getting cursed to live as a hobo has its positives.'

Poppy rolled the information over in her mind before realising that if she could accept him being a werewolf then she could accept his inability to age.

'So if you're in the school, I may get to see you around.'

'Maybe.' He glanced up and shrugged. 'But we can't talk much more, they're looking for you.'

In the distance she could hear the distant calls of her name and she sighed in frustration. 'It's like they think I'm made of glass.'

'Don't knock it. At least they care.' He got up from the log and began to walk away.

'Nicholas?'

'I can't be seen by everyone. I'm not a tame werewolf. I keep people safe by being away from them.'

'Will I see you again?'

'Maybe.' He glanced back over his shoulder. 'But try not to fall down any holes in the future.'

'I …' She was distracted by the shout of her name and when she looked back, he had gone.

As her friends reached her side and began to fuss, she wondered if she would see him again and whether he could return to the world. After all, he had saved her life, maybe she could save his.

SCARLETT

'A little bit more adventurous, darling,' Raiker's voice crackled through the communications implant. 'Some acrobatics if you would.'

Scarlett didn't reply, save to reach for the rings that were above her. As she moved deeper into the routine for this particular piece of music, she tried not to focus on the ground below. Suspended a full thirty feet above the dance floor in a clear box, Scarlett threw herself into her job. It was three a.m. and the writhing mass of bodies below showed no sign of slowing. As her body twirled and performed, her skin flared with an almost translucent glow which she controlled with a stray thought.

Scarlett, like most of the dancers at The Sweet Spot, was laced with cosmetic alteration. In her case, the cyberware that traced through her body dealt with light. Hair and skin laced with artificial pigments that changed colour with a thought. She shifted into a difficult, upside-down pose and her hair shone with a purple light as flowers bloomed across her skin like living tattoos.

'That's perfect, sweetheart.' Raiker shifted the music to something ethereal and slow, the club light shifted to a soft gold.

In the pale light, her hair and body shone above the dance floor like a beacon. Scarlett closed her eyes and drifted into the sound.

'Just one more and then you're out of there for tonight.'

Scarlett nodded and continued to hang above the floor, flexing and twirling in mid-air as her muscles protested the strain. Her hair streamed across her face as the purple glow danced across her skin. It felt strangely free to be hovering above the dancefloor held by nothing but her own body weight. Flowing notes of music caressed her ears and she smiled as her muscles followed the music in effortless motion. In these moments her past life was far away as though it were a dream.

'And you're done.' Raiker's voice brought her back as the ethereal, trancelike music faded and segued into a pulsing heavy dance beat.

Scarlett caught hold of the ladder and started to climb out of the box. On the gantry, she faced Misty who flashed a nervous smile before she descended into the now empty box.

The noise from the dance floor dwindled as Scarlett headed backstage. Raiker had invested heavily in sound-proofing for the dressing rooms and it provided a welcome respite from the noise of the club. White noise flew from speakers and she began to relax, switching off her implants as she grabbed the nearest towel.

'Shower's free,' Lace called as she walked through the dressing room.

'Thanks.' Scarlett began to peel the outfit from her skin. Beneath the cold lights of the dressing room the cybernetic implants looked like pale tattoos against her dusky skin. She stepped out of the red body suit, the fabric somehow dull and mundane after the lights of the club. Raking a hand through hair that was damp with sweat, Scarlett padded naked for the shower.

'Good job tonight,' Lace spoke again, her rich voice admiring over the noise of the water. She leaned against the bathroom door. 'I don't know how you manage to do all that up there.'

'It's good if you don't think about it,' Scarlett replied from beneath the spray. 'You're usually on the main stage and I couldn't do that.'

'What cyberware do you have?'

'Optics and the usual netware.' She began to wash her hair, which acted very much like real hair. 'Performance stuff.' She rinsed off the suds and stepped out of the shower. Taking the towel, she wrapped herself in the soft fabric and drew level with the other woman. 'You?'

'Headwear and audio enhancement.' Lace lifted her black locks to show off a plug at the base of her neck. 'It's useful.'

Scarlett shrugged and started to walk past the other woman, her thoughts becoming jumbled. Lace was new to the Sweet Spot and a performer with only audio adjustments didn't make sense. She turned and ran her gaze over the other girl, noting her athletic build and the minute scars that traced across her body and a chill crept up her spine. Whatever else she was, Lace was no more a performer than she was an archivist.

She reached the dressing room and finished towelling off. Lace followed her from the bathroom and watched as she began to dress. The stare was calculating, measuring, as though Lace were ticking off an invisible checklist. It could have been desire, yet Scarlett didn't think so. The girl's stare was cool, efficient and, despite the apparent friendliness of her tone, ruthless. Now in the empty calm of the dressing room she could see what she had missed over the last few days.

Buried beneath the façade of a performer was the cold determination of a hunter and a chill settled into Scarlett's bones. She tried not to panic, there was no guarantee that Lace was here for her, but that felt more like wishful thinking than anything else.

'How long have you worked here?' The question sounded light, idly curious, but Scarlett could feel the intent behind it.

'Five years.' Scarlett dragged on a pair of black leggings as she began to connect a call to Raiker. There had been hunters sent to infiltrate them before but none of the others had succeeded in staying longer than a day. 'Been a lightbox dancer for all that time.' White noise surged through her communicator preventing the call from connecting, yet she continued to chat as though the other girl were only a fellow dancer.

'Must be fun.' A small smile touched the corners of the other girl's mouth as her cybernetic eyes located the small birthmark on the curvature of her spine.

It was a quick glance, not of any note, and yet in that simple look Scarlett knew that she was in trouble. She had thought in the last five years that she was now safe, hidden from those looking for her and now, with that casual, almost flirting look, Lace had dispelled her illusions.

Scarlett reached for her blouse as casually as she could beneath the other girl's stare. She couldn't let Lace know that she was onto her. With Raiker out of contact and no one else in the dressing room Scarlett was alone. 'Sometimes it is.' She stopped speaking as Lace stepped towards her and her fingers froze on the buttons of her blouse.

'I can tell.' Another step and Lace was an arm's length away. 'Do I make you nervous?' Another smile creased her lips and Scarlett resisted the temptation to step back.

'A little.' Admitting to a small amount of fear gave her some sense of balance as she attempted to clear the channels on her headset.

'And why might that be?' The girl reached her and fingers settled against her upper arm. Heat blazed with the touch of her fingers and Scarlett only just managed to hold back her yelp of pain. Any reaction would confirm Lace's suspicions and she had only to keep her busy until help came.

'It's just I … I …' She thought quickly, feverishly, as she hoped that Lace hadn't left an imprint on her skin. 'I quite like you but I didn't think you were interested.' It was a last-ditch, Hail Mary prayer and she hoped she could pull off the bluff enough to get through to Raiker.

Lace stopped moving and stared at her in shock. 'You think I'm …?' She started again, this time allowing an indulgent smile to cross her lips. 'You think I'm coming onto you?'

'Aren't you?' Scarlett began to gabble, hoping to bury her real fears beneath false ones. 'I mean, I'm flattered and all and I won't lie and say I haven't been interested. But you could be a little less stalkery with it."

Once again, she tried for Raiker and this time connected.

Hunter in the dressing room

She sent the message swiftly as she continued to babble hoping to gain some more time. 'I mean, you're gorgeous and all, but you are coming across as a little creepy.'

Lace laughed, a rich, throaty chuckle that echoed through the room. 'Well, there's a reason for that.' Her other hand reached out and burning fingers settled against Scarlett's upper arm. 'And you know why.' The heat in her fingers increased and Scarlett couldn't stop the yelp of pain from between her lips.

The other girl's face split into a wide, satisfied smile. 'And there you are.'

Scarlett tried to pull away but Lace held on fast.

'Traitor.' Lace hissed.

The pain raced through the skin on her arms, activating the long-buried cyberware beneath her skin. The newly-acquired light wave tech flared once as their circuits blazed out and died, killed by older and stronger technology. Scarlett screamed as she felt the muscle lacing snap into place and begin to lock. She knew this move. The other girl had activated a capture function buried deep within the older technology and she was helpless to stop her limbs from forcing her into a kneeling position.

'Get off me.' Scarlett snarled as she tried to connect with the cyberware, attempting to break Lace's control. Prickles of fire raced within her as long-forgotten connections began to charge beneath her skin. It had been five years since she had activated the lacing embedded in her skin and the pain was almost unbearable as the systems flared back into existence.

As Lace moved in to lock her arms into position, the pain eased. She straightened up, the capture function failing as an override erased the new instructions.

'I said,' Scarlett's voice was soft yet a steely determination had replaced the anger. 'Get off me.'

She twisted and kicked, her leg moving at a speed that was beyond humanly possible. Lace blocked the strike and went on the defensive, the smile dropping from her face as two sharp blades locked into place along Scarlett's forearms.

They paced about each other in the small space, eyes measuring each move looking for weaknesses. Scarlett hadn't needed to use her implants for some time but she was under no illusions that she could hold her own indefinitely. She only had to hold on until Raiker got here.

She dived to the side as Lace attacked, her kinetically-enhanced reflexes barely giving a hint of movement. Shaking her head briefly before ducking again, Scarlett tried to remember old moves and holds, wishing that she had maintained her own systems in the years since she had left the Guild.

She slashed out with her left blade and followed up with the right, moving in an attack pattern that she thought had been erased. With the capture function disabled, Lace had no choice but to retaliate. A knee slammed into her stomach as her blades sliced deeply into Lace's upper arms. A spark of electricity escaped from the cuts and Scarlett's stomach flipped as she realised that the other girl was more cyber than human. As she took in that information, blades slid into place on Lace's wrists, sparkling with blue energy.

It was a matter of survival now. Even with the cyberware in her system, she couldn't hold out for long against someone with that much modification. A kick to the knees followed with two slashes towards the abdomen and Lace backed off, finding it difficult to manoeuvre in the small room. As Scarlett pressed the advantage, Lace attacked, forcing her to stagger back to avoid the arcing energy blades.

'Like them?' They missed her nose by mere milimetres as Lace spoke. 'They can slice through cyberlimbs like hot knives through butter.'

Scarlett didn't answer, unwilling to waste energy on something as pointless as talking when avoiding those blades took up most of her attention. She ducked the next blow and aimed another kick at Lace's side only to feel nothing but air as the other girl slipped to one side.

'Too slow.' The blade hissed through the air and connected with her upper arm. Scarlett screamed as fire raced across her skin while the blue-edged blade severed the connections to her cyberware. With one arm falling uselessly to her side, she ducked the next blow, flailing uselessly with her other arm. The blade struck again, this time to her side and she fell against one of the cushioned seats.

'You should have just let me shut you down.' Lace leant over her with a smirk. 'It would have been easier.' The flickering blue edges of the blades crept closer to her throat. 'Traitorous bitch.' Scarlett felt the heat from the blades and she inched backwards. 'The guild is for life, don't you know that?'

'Oh yes,' she snarled back. 'Wait until they ask you to kill the man you love and see if you can take the order so easily.' Pain exploded across her cheek as Lace laid the edge of a blade against her skin.

'The guild said to take you back, but ...' Lace forced her head up. 'I can't be bothered with that.'

She moved her hand back to strike a finishing blow but the blade didn't fall. Instead a strange burbling noise came from her mouth as her body froze in place. Behind Lace, Raiker walked across the dressing room floor, a small box in his hand. His eyes were free of his usual contacts and shone golden amber in the dressing room light. They were signs of his mutation and the kill order that Scarlett could not deliver. In the final analysis she would always follow her love.

'Get a move on, darling. I can't hold her forever.'

Scarlett got to her feet and brought her one good arm up to the other girl's neck. 'I wish I could say I was better than this, but ...' She brought her blade down and severed Lace's carotid artery. 'I can't have you following us.'

Leaving Lace to fall behind her, she reached Raiker's side as she sheathed the blades. They shared a quick, passionate kiss. 'We'd better go. Where there's one ...'

'There's more.' He handed her a coat and picked up that night's takings. 'Damn shame.' Raiker caught hold of her hand as they headed for the back door. 'I was beginning to enjoy this life.' The door opened into a rainy London night lit by neon.

'But living would be better.'

He nodded as he tenderly pulled a hood over her head. 'I've booked us tickets for the early train for Paris.'

'Then we'd better go.'

They let the door slam behind them as they walked along the street, blending easily with the nightlife.

JANE HOOD - DIARIST

Monday

Once upon a time … yes, I know it's stupid to begin a tale with that, but I really can't help myself. After all I am the product of all of that happily-ever-after rubbish. My parents are Red Riding Hood and the Woodsman. Yeah, I have the wonderfully double-barrelled surname of Woodsman-Hood. Why they saddled me with that is anyone's guess. My forename is the extremely dull, boring-as-soap moniker of Jane. So, I have a long surname that should really belong with a fancy forename but instead I wind up with Jane. I guess my mother got hacked off with all the 'Red' jokes that she had to put up with over the years. My father stopped being a woodsman after the wolf thing and he's now a hunter tracking down the vicious werewolves that try to eat grannies and little girls walking through the wood. You may notice that I'm not really impressed. Yes, my father cut up the wolf and dragged my mum out of his belly, which is quite awesome, unfortunately his wolf cutting list has stuck on one for the last few years and all he seems to bag are regular, common as muck, wolves. Yes, I know I sound like an ungrateful brat, but really, how can you trade on the reputation of one dead werewolf for so many years?

Anyway, with that out of the way, I'd like to draw your attention to my little village. It's about two miles away and I get to walk that every day. So, I'm fit and have no friends. Literally every other kid at school lives in the town, but not us … oh no … we have to live in the middle of nowhere. So naturally I don't get visitors and I can't go to someone else's house after school. Life is literally walk to school, school, walk home from school, tea and then bed. I almost wish to meet a wolf in the woods, so that at least my life would be a little more interesting.

Tuesday

Not a great deal to report today. We did get a couple of new kids at school. Brother and sister, Hansel and Gretel. Both exceptionally attractive, but not stuck up with it and the best bit is they live about half a mile from us. Maybe some friends at last.

Wednesday

Spoke to Gretel today, and I've no idea what happened to me. She's the most attractive girl at my school and for some bizarre reason I just couldn't form a sentence. She looked at me with those big brown eyes and I just … well … mumbled something incoherent. God, she must think I'm an idiot. Must make a better impression tomorrow.

Thursday

Better impression made. Had a five-minute conversation about living in the woods (we both hate it, by the way) and discussed maths homework. She loaned me a pencil, which was very nice of her and suggested that we walk some of the way to school together. Hansel joined us, of course, and he's just as cute as his sister.

Friday
Saturday
Sunday

Far too much homework to add much.

Monday

One of the smaller children went missing in the woods this morning. I heard Mum and Dad talking about it before I left for school. They insisted I take a dagger with me. I figured I'd be okay walking with those two, but I took the dagger anyway. I hope that little kid is okay. . Started to walk with Hansel and Gretel to school. Gretel's really sweet, but there's this... I don't know...oddness to her. I offered her a bit of gingerbread and she practically freaked. She apologised really fast, but you would have thought I was trying to poison her.

Tuesday

Homework tonight and Gretel came over for tea. She brought this apple strudel thing for my Mum and immediately became her favourite person. Also, she's better at maths than I am, so ... great for copying. We spoke about that missing boy and she seemed very worried. I think it's because she's closer to the woods. Dad's gone out hunting for the boy and he's defaulted back to wolf blaming.

Wednesday

They still haven't found him and another kid has vanished. This one was closer to town. All of us have been told to walk in groups.

Thursday

Hansel is ill, so Gretel and I walked to school alone. She's got a great sense of humour; I think I prefer her company to her brother. Still no sign of missing kids.

Saturday

They found the first boy… and I just can't think about it. Dad's gone on a wolf hunt and the rest of the village is talking about hiring soldiers. No-one's allowed to walk alone. It's getting scary and I don't know what to do. Luckily, I have friends now. Gretel came to visit today and we just did homework and talked about school stuff. It got a little awkward when we spoke about boys. I've never really thought about them, they all seem like immature prats to me. Gretel seemed to get it though. I know a lot of the guys think she's pretty, but she seemed as uninterested in all that as I am. It's strange but when she laughs, I feel really happy and I just want to get a little closer. I keep wondering if she thinks of me when I'm not there.

Sunday

Church was an interesting experience. Vicar went on full "kill the beasts" mode and declared a curfew. This means that I will have to leave school really early in order to get home. Mum gave me her red hood coat to wear, which doesn't fill me full of confidence. Let's face it, wearing a bright red cape didn't exactly save her from a wolf. Walked home with both Hansel and Gretel and got talking about famous families; after all, Red Hood and Woodsman. Turns out they're quite famous as well. They were nearly killed by a witch in a gingerbread house, which of course explains the fear of gingerbread.

Gretel was all shades of awesome during that adventure apparently. She won the day and saved both their lives. She burned the witch to death in an oven and managed to get her brother out of a cage.

We thought we heard howling as we walked back, so we ran the rest of the way home.

Monday

I don't know what to think or do. I mean, I guess it's a good thing. I keep thinking about it and it was really, really great but what if she says something? What if she's having a joke and didn't mean it? What if she never speaks to me again? It was absolutely epic and it made me feel so wonderful but now I'm freaking out and so worried I just can't …

I guess I should explain because I've just re-read that and it doesn't make sense. So …

Gretel came over again without her brother. Apparently, he had other things to do. I didn't mind, while he *is* cute, I really prefer Gretel's company. So, we went to my room, did the normal stuff like homework and gossiped about the kids at school while trying to avoid the subject of missing people. And then it got ~~weird~~ different. We were talking about boys and kissing and it was real awkward 'cos absolutely no guy has asked me out before and I felt a little stupid. But she asked if I had ever been … you know … kissed? I said no and she asked, "Do you want to?" Well, I was ~~interested~~ totally fascinated and it was just a kiss, so I leaned in and … diary, I think I've worked out why I'm not interested in a lot of the boys at school. It was amazing and I was so nervous. I mean, it might not mean anything to her, but I keep thinking about kissing her again. It wasn't just a peck either, it kind of started as a peck, but something fizzed between us and we properly kissed. She nibbled my lip and I felt like dying. If it hadn't been for Mum calling us for tea, we would still be there.

After she went home though, I felt really bad. And now I'm freaking out. What if she was only playing? What if she tells everyone? They already think I'm a bit of a freak at school and this … well … this could be all kinds of hell. Wondering if I should pretend to be sick in the morning.

Tuesday

I worried for nothing. I spent all of last night tossing and turning and panicking and this morning she made me feel so much better about it. She took my hand and apologised if she made me uncomfortable. I said she hadn't and we held hands all the way to school. I felt so relieved and happy that I didn't even worry at the distant howl we heard on the way there.

There was a special assembly when we got there; they've found the second body and we've all been sent home. Mr Draylott, the headteacher, gave me and Gretel a note for our parents. Turns out they want us to move into town where it's a little more crowded and safer.

Wednesday

Mr Draylott was attacked in his house last night, he's not dead but his housekeeper raised the alarm. Mine and Gretel's parents collected us for the walk home today. We're not moving into town, but we are all moving into our house for protection. Gretel gets to share my room 'cos of course, "girls wouldn't get up to any funny business." If only they knew of my fantasies with Gretel in my room all night.

Thursday

Well, my fantasies took a blow yesterday; we didn't get any time together last night. Dad had us practicing with weapons damn near all night. We kept hearing shouts from the militia and howls from the forest and I began to get a little freaked. Maybe we should move into town. Dad handed me this massive crossbow and started showing me how to use it. I may have been a little hasty at declaring him past it. Gretel is a natural at throwing knifes and maybe we can protect ourselves but it certainly made us tired. We didn't get any talking done or anything else as we fell asleep as soon as we got upstairs. Hoping that will change in the next few nights.

Friday

It's two in the morning and I'm writing this in case we all end up dead. There was a large bang about fifteen minutes ago which woke us all up. All of the adults are now in the living room having barricaded the door and Hansel, Gretel and I are currently in the dining room. Nobody's talking much but I can hear sounds in the garden, I think they're trying to get in. Oh fuck, something's banging on the front door …

Saturday

Sunday

Monday

Tuesday

I don't know what to say … I don't know what to do. Something was trying to get in but the front door was too heavy or something and the next thing we knew, this huge wolf burst in through the window. Hansel was right in front of the window and several large pieces of glass sliced into him. He's okay and he tried to fight off the wolf but couldn't keep it away. Then it came for Gretel and me. We shot it but all it did was make it angry and then it clawed at Gretel. She fell over and there was so much blood. I just couldn't leave them. I heard Dad coming up the stairs and I picked up one of the crossbow bolts. It's all a bit of a blur then. I remember it coming at me and I remember the pain as it clawed at my leg. There was so much shouting and then agony. I can't remember what happened next, only I woke up today and the healer's changing my bandages. When Dad saw me, he looked so choked up and could barely speak. I've got claw marks all down my arm and some more on my upper shoulder which would be okay except for the bite mark on my hip. My mum hasn't stopped crying and Gretel's parents have dragged her away. The vicar hasn't stopped praying since I woke up and when they think I'm asleep I hear them talking. They think I'm turning into a werewolf and they don't know what to do. We wounded the one that bit me and he ran away. They're hoping that they managed to clean the bite in time but they don't know. Mum's tying so much silver about me that I can barely stand up and at least one of the villagers is discussing whether I should be allowed to live.

What's worst is that Gretel and I have barely spoken. I saw her briefly before her mum turned up and took her away and I'm scared that we'll never get to do anything more than that pretend kiss we shared.

Wednesday

They let me out today but you'd think I was dead. No one is talking to me. No one even comes close. Mothers chase their children in when they see me coming and the new headteacher hasn't let me go back to school. They're scared and I can't blame them, I'm scared too.

Thursday

Gretel's mum slammed the door in my face when I tried to see her. I don't know if Gretel knew I was there but I saw Hansel and though he tried to come to the door, his mum stopped him.

Friday

Gretel's been kept at home. Her family have locked both of them in the house. My parents are barely any better. Mum asked me to stay indoors while they look up the options. I don't think I've ever worried so much about that phrase before.

Saturday

I don't think I can take this isolation. All Mum does is cry and Dad is busy looking at werewolf lore. I think he's worried that he'll be asked to kill me. No one is laughing in our house anymore and I'm so lonely I could cry.

Sunday

The mayor turned up today. As it's the full moon tomorrow, I'm to be locked in the jail and watched in case I turn. No one has said what will happen to me if I do.

Monday

Gretel managed to visit me today. She was allowed into my cell and we kissed properly for the first time. She says her mother is scared that I'll hurt her. Well, I'm scared that I'll hurt her and I told her to go home. She's braver than me and wanted to stay. The sun's going down and the guard have reinforced the doors. Gretel is still there watching me and I think she's the one. But what if I change?

Tuesday

I became the wolf. And now they're debating my fate. I guess Dad's sorry about all of that wolf business now. I didn't hurt anyone and all of the locks held, so it's possible that I could be controlled. But, to hear the vicar call it, I'm a vicious monster that must be killed. Gretel stayed with me the whole time and apparently, I calmed down when she spoke, so maybe I remember something of my real life when I change. They're locking me in again tonight but I notice that they're building gallows in the town square. Father is angry and Mum cries. Me, I don't know what to do.

Wednesday

They pronounced sentence on me this morning and I'm to be killed before the sun sets tonight.

Gretel has promised that I won't die. I don't know what

she can do. But I don't want to be a monster like the one who killed those children.

(written in another hand and undated)

I don't know how to finish this book, to see her hopes and dreams before they faded. I fell in love with her humour, her nature and we never got further than stolen kisses. All I know is her ending. They took her to the gallows and put the noose round her neck. Her father caused a scene and, as they were distracted, my brother and I set her free. She had to run, to head into the forest and be safe. My parents are outraged, but we did the right thing. I never got the chance to see her again. Maybe she died out there or maybe she steers clear of people. She never wanted to be evil.

I left that village the summer following and joined the Silver Charter. They're a band of werewolf hunters but they try to cure the affliction and only offer death if requested by the cursed. We're chasing a lead now into the wilds and I think it's the creature that initially terrorised our village. There's lore that states that those turned can be cured with the death of their creator. If it is true, then she may finally be free. And then I can find her and we can begin the life we should have had.

THE GREAT HUNT

The late October sun hung low in the sky as the Hunt song echoed from the town walls. The feast was being prepared and from my huddled place in the straw I could almost follow the movements of my fellow villagers. The village women would be chattering as they prepared wreaths of night blossom and ivy. If all had gone well, I would have been with them, weaving the same wreaths and waiting for the town men to return from the forest. The scent of roasting meat would rise from the fire and drink and food would flow till dawn. But that was last year.

The heavy steps of the town magistrate echoed along the corridor outside of my cell and I stood up, unwilling to remain cowed in the corner like some rabbit. As the noise of keys rattled in the lock, I thought back over the evening and the reason for my punishment.

'It's barbaric.' Kayla had whispered as she flicked through the woodcuts of last year's hunt. 'You wouldn't find this insult occurring in town.'

'You don't understand it,' I had replied in the same, quiet tones, unwilling to let the priest hear our words. 'It's a tradition and a party.' I didn't like the way that Kayla dismissed our little village but as she was one of the more popular girls at school, I couldn't just ignore her. Her friendship made travelling to the nearby town less lonely.

'A bunch of men stumbling through the woods chasing after a girl.' She shrugged her shoulders with distaste. 'And what do they do when they catch her?'

'Nothing untoward.' I hissed back. 'She has to escape or be caught.' I gave a small chuckle. 'Last year Annie Goodman got caught in the first ten minutes. They had to let her go again or the food wouldn't have been ready.'

'Still superstitious nonsense.'

'What is?' We had jumped as Father Lawrence's voice interrupted our whispered conversation.

'This hunt.' Kayla had had no shame as she faced down the Priest. 'No one does this thing anymore.'

'And the land suffers for it,' Father Lawrence had replied with a mild, disapproving tone. 'Men like your father replace reverence for the land with the cold love of gold.'

'Yes, of course.' I had tried to step on her foot but she was too far from me. 'A bonfire and a fake hunt will keep the harvest on time.' She had dropped the bunch of woodcuts. 'Come on, Garnet.'

'Garnet.' I glanced up as the 'dour face of the priest filled the doorway. 'Time to go, child.'

Behind him stood the four leaders of the hunt and a chill ran down my spine. I barely recognised the men who were my neighbours, masked as they were. A strange thrill buzzed beneath my skin.

Jorunn, no, he was not Jorunn this evening, stepped forward with a small engraved pot in his fingers. The stopper was a single jewel, its sides smooth from countless years of use, blood-red and glittering. My namesake winked at me in the light before it came free in burly fingers.

'Take it.' Jorunn held out the pot and my fingers slowly made their way to the red, fragrant dust within. My fingers drifted across my arms tracing the lines of quarry that I knew by rote.

'Drink.' Skel passed the wineskin and I took a hefty swallow, feeling the warmth of the concoction burn down my throat and fortify my nerves.

'So, it's your turn this year?' Kayla's voice had rippled with scorn. 'How can you put up with it?'

'I'm not being forced to marry or anything. It's only a bit of fun.'

'Really?' Kayla had pushed me back against the wall and pushed a scrap of paper into my hands. 'That says that a girl died one year.' Another scrap of paper. 'And that one talks of assault.'

'That girl fell down a hill in the dark and the other girl I've not heard of. There's certainly been no one of that name on the hunt before …'

'Why am I even talking to you? You're just an idiotic, country bumpkin,' Kayla had sniffed as she pulled back. 'And I thought you had brains.'

I watched her walk away with feelings of panic. Kayla was

practically the only girl of my age in the village and if I lost her as a friend ...

'Wait a minute ...' I had called. Kayla had turned back to face me with an expectant look on her face. 'I'll come with you.' I glanced down at the parchment. 'Maybe it is a little bit foolish.'

'Wear.' Mal pushed an old, matted bundle of fur into my arms and I pulled on the coat, feeling once more the strange thrill that only just bubbled beneath the fear.

They flanked me on all sides, their bulk threatening in small cell of the jail. I followed their steady tread out into the clear, frosty air. Unlike other years there were no cheers or mockery. Today was silent and full of gravity. My mother could be seen on the other side of the clearing yet she gave no sign of encouragement. My crime had doomed her most of all.

'Look, I'll prove it to you.' Kayla had stood outside of the shrine with a mocking smile on her features. 'Take that.' She pointed to the craven mask that stood amid the wealth of offerings.

I stepped back, real concern in my voice. 'It's forbidden.' The wolf mask had stayed there since the last hunt and was not to be touched. It was even off-limits from the younger boys' games of dare.

'Chicken.' Kayla had reached out a hand and took hold of the carved image lifting it from its spot. I felt a tremor race through me as she brought the mask to her face. 'It's not even well-made.'

'Speak.' Kael's guttural voice finished the ritual, his hair not quite hidden by the bird's feathers that surrounded his mask.

I took a breath and the words tumbled from my lips in perfect time and tempo. The words that I had been desperate to avoid. 'I offer myself to the Hunt, to the chase. To the cut of blood and the dance till death. I will lead the Hunt to the end of the night and they will suffer in my dust.' A strange thrill raced down my skin as I fixed the buttons on the front of the coat, the fear leaving me as the symbols of the Hunt settled into place.

'You shall run through the forest and meadow.' The priest approached, the mask in his hands different from the others. This mask, held high in his arms, was darker and more primal than the one usually used. This was a mask of solemnity and tradition, a mask of sacrifice. 'Along the stream and into the dell.' Ruddy light from the fire sent flickering shadows over the wicked visage and I swallowed nervously. 'You will run till you escape or till you die or till you take a life.' A sigh echoed across the ground, the words different from those before. 'Until you atone for your sin.'

'Stop!' I had reached out for the mask, attempting to seize it from her hands, suddenly afraid that others would see. 'You can't.'

'It's all nonsense.' She had wrenched it back and the mask fell to the ground, the ancient stone shattering in a shower of dust and grit. As the shards flew into the air, a howl like all the wolves in the world shrilled about us. Kayla grabbed hold of my arms, fear replacing the mockery in an instant. 'What is it?'

'What have you done?' I hunched down to look at the shattered remnants of the mask, horror thrumming through me. 'You've destroyed it.'

From the village I could hear the sounds of running footsteps and I glanced back as Kayla pitched to her knees in a faint. As the rest of the village raced into view, I had stared down at the broken mask and tried to work out what to say.

He bound the mask to my head and stepped back. I held out my hand and a knife stabbed into my thumb sending drops of blood to the dark earth. As instructed, I drew the blood to the mask and smeared it across the grinning maw of a mouth. As the drops of rich crimson passed the teeth, I could hear the beginnings of a prayer from the Priest, a prayer full of entreaty and darkness. The words were taken up by others, the ancient words redolent with meaning. These were different words than normal, but then this was no normal Hunt.

Beneath the dying light of an Autumn sky something primal began to throb beneath my skin, something that replaced the fear.

'I run …' I felt powerful as the strange magic of this costume began its work. My voice carried through the crowd to my parents and they straightened up, a small smile of encouragement finally entering their gaze. 'I hunt.' The pain in my thumb began to recede as my eyesight seemed to sharpen, picking out each face in the crowd and Kayla's still form, laid on a stone bier before the fire. She had not woken since the shattering of the idol.

The four men knelt before me, firelight shining off muscle-bound, naked torsos, yet I sneered down at them. The magic was altering my senses and warping my thoughts. How could I have been so afraid of these? These men were nothing and I would leave them in the dust.

My senses seemed sharper despite the cumbersome mask that I wore and I sniffed the air experimentally, tasting the loam and life of the forest. I could feel my mind drift into the background, leaving instinct in its place. An instinct I only now recognised. I could feel the garments shift about me, moulding closer to my body as the marks on my arms shimmered.

'I kill.' My words rippled through the crowd like a shot and I smiled, the mask more my face than the skin beneath. As the last rays of the sun disappeared beneath the trees, I raised my head and howled to the sky, my voice finally no longer human.

I was the hunter; I was the prey. With a prowess I did not know I possessed, I sprang into action and raced for the bier. The desecrator lay there, asleep and lost. A cruel smile crossed my lips as I brought my arm down, my newly-grown claws ending her life in an instant. As the crowd stepped back in shock, I howled once more and raced for the edge of the forest, the blood pounding through my head like a drum as each of the hunters took chase.

HOME

'Stay away from that window.' Rose jerked back from the frosted glass at her grandmother's harsh voice. 'What have I told you about sitting so close during the Winter?'

'Not to look at the snow.'

It was a lesson that had been drilled into her throughout her life. A lesson punctuated with stories about Frost Fairies and Winter Spirits, and warnings about drawing down their attention. Rose moved away from the window and settled back against the cushioned chair as she glanced across at the door leading to her father's room. Every Winter, her father secluded himself away from the family. She knew that he sat at the window and stared into the wintry darkness, but Grandmother said little about that.

Whatever weighed on her father during the Winter months made him sob in his sleep and once, just once, she had heard a name spoken. Geada. Grandmother had sent Rose to her room refusing to answer any of her questions and returned to her father, waking him with soft admonishments and reassurances.

During the rest of the year her father was hale and hearty with no sign of care and yet, at this time of year, when the freezing wind tugged at the eaves and snow fell in fluffy drifts about the door, her father fell into a depression she could not fathom or understand. Though she knew it had something to do with her mother. She bent over the crochet in her lap and sighed as she thought of that mystery. Father never spoke of her and Grandmother grew angry whenever Rose brought the subject up. Her Aunt Katherine was the best bet for information but she had a family of her own and now lived in town.

So, Rose had to guess as to her mother's identity. All she knew is that her mother had left her as a baby on the doorstep and then vanished into the snowy night like a ghost. Maybe her mother could explain her colouring. Her father and grandmother were dark-haired and ruddy with exposure to the elements yet her skin was so pale it was almost translucent. Blue eyes the colour of an ice floe glimmered beneath unruly blue-black locks. People in the town said she looked cold even through the Summer months yet she never seemed to feel it. Her differences were clear to all with eyes and her grandmother refused to answer any of her questions regarding them.

The fire popped and hissed as it ate at the wood stacked in its hearth and Rose backed away from its warmth preferring the cooler parts of the room. That was something else Grandmother complained about – her like of the cold and

frost. Summer made her listless and she spent hours during hot, sleepy afternoons laid in the glacial cold waters of the creek.

The wind increased and rattled the door handle, causing her grandmother to glance sharply at the portal as though she expected the wind to attack her. Rose however felt no concern. It was purely the bitter Winter wind and nothing she would be concerned about. If anything, it felt more welcoming than the cheery fire in the grate.

'Geada.'

Rose looked up at the sound of her father's voice. He had left his room and now stood in the centre of the small living room. Mismatched socks hung loosely from his feet, the stumps of missing toes clearly visible and a thick woollen jumper covered his nightshirt. A lost, hopeless look ghosted through his eyes and Rose felt her stomach clench at the frail shell of the man before her.

'Athan ...' Grandmother stood up and reached for her son. 'Go back to bed, my son.' A soft, tormented note entered her voice as her fingers settled on his upper arm.

'No, Mother.' He peeled her fingers away from his skin. 'My Geada's come back to me ... I heard her ...'

Rose bent her head over her crochet, hiding her tears. She hated seeing her father like this, hated seeing him so anguished. What had her mother done to him?

'You didn't hear anything,' Grandmother snapped back. 'Just the Winter wind ...'

'I saw her at the edge of the clearing,' her father insisted as he pulled away from his mother's grasp. 'She came back, just as I knew she would.' The wind rattled the door again and its mournful wail echoed through the room. 'I told you, Mother.' His gaze flickered across the room to rest on Rose. 'She's come back for Rose.'

'And she certainly can't have her.' Stern, angry words, in stark contrast to the pity seen before seared across the room. 'She destroyed you and I'm not letting the same thing happen to my granddaughter.'

Rose watched with alarm as her grandmother strode to the door and drew another bolt across the wood.

'She won't hurt her, Mother ...'

'Like she didn't hurt you?' Pity mixed with derision flowed through her voice as another bolt slid home. 'You're not whole, my son, and it's her fault. I'll be damned it I let her take the only thing she left you with.'

'Why, Grandma?' Rose pushed aside the crochet and stood up, butterflies churning unpleasantly in her stomach. 'What did my mother do?'

Silence settled on the small room and her grandmother gave a sigh, her gnarled fingers still resting against the solid bulk of the door. 'It's nothing for you to concern yourself about, child.'

'Why can't you just tell me instead of talking in riddles?' Heat flared beneath her skin and her head began to throb. Outside the wind increased in tempo and her grandmother glanced up with concern. 'I'm tired of being treated like a child.'

'You are a child.' Her grandmother drew herself up to her full height. 'And you don't need to know these things.'

'But they're about me.' Rose tried to hold onto her temper. 'What about my mother? Who is she?'

'She …' Her father began, but her grandmother cut him off with a slash of her hand.

'No, Athan. She does not need to know.'

'Why not?' Confusion and anger whipped through her thoughts as she took a pace forward. 'It's my mother.'

'And no good will come of the knowing.' A crooked finger waved in her father's direction. 'See what she did to your father. I'm damned if I'll let her hooks get into you.'

'I'm old enough to decide that.'

The window rattled in the frame and her grandmother cast a worried look at it. Rose glanced out into snowy darkness, sure that she had seen a figure drift across the glass.

'No, you are still a child.' Her grandmother stood and folded her arms across her chest. 'You do not need to know about her.'

'Fine.' Rose threw the crochet to one side and flounced off towards her small room on the other side of the house. 'Keep it from me. I'll ask Auntie Katherine.'

'Your aunt won't say anything if she knows what's good for her.' Her grandmother's voice followed her as she slammed the door.

Rose did not respond as she threw herself across her bed and stared at the oil lamp. Her room was the only one without windows, though at some point they had existed. The frames were still visible in the wall. It was as though her grandmother meant to keep from looking at the woods during Winter.

Through the closed door, she could hear her grandmother coax her father back to his room and she huffed a sigh of frustration. That conversation had contained the most information Athan had ever imparted about her mother and her grandmother had stopped it.

As the wind rattled the eaves she decided to wait until the house was asleep and glance out of the window in defiance of her grandmother's rules. If she wouldn't tell her about her mother, then she would find out for herself. The noise of the wind calmed her and she settled back against the pillow determined to walk to Aunt Katherine's in the morning and discover the truth for herself, for her father would never be able to tell her whilst his mother watched like a hawk.

* * *

The lights in the cabin had been dimmed and quiet had settled over its occupants as Rose quietly crept from her bed to the window. Carefully she drew back the drapes and pressed her nose up against the cool glass. Her breath misted the rough-blown surface and she wiped it away as her eyes travelled over the snowy field and the dark trees beyond.

Snow drifted in the wind, its crystals catching the moonlight as it flowed like a lady's cape in the wind. Beyond the drifts she could see the boughs of naked oaks, stark and weighted down with snow and she sighed, the beauty holding her transfixed as always. A small flurry of snowflakes danced before the window and her fingers drifted across the cold glass following the flakes that seemed to dance in the wake of her hand.

Sniggering slightly at her fancies, she raised her finger and traced it in a circle expecting the flurry to settle onto the sill but they did not. She froze as the flakes circled in the air before her, lazily dancing as though the wind beyond did not affect them. Shaking her head, she traced the circle in the opposite direction and stifled a yelp as the snow followed. Closing her hand, she backed away from the window determined to climb back into bed and normality when a voice drifted through her mind.

Come to me, my daughter.

She froze and glanced back to the window. Beyond the glass and in the centre of the clearing stood a woman of silver and frost. A woman of Winter and chill. Her mother? A pale hand beckoned her forward and she grit her teeth warnings from her grandmother running through her mind. This was a Winter Spirit, it couldn't be her mother and yet … She remembered her affinity to cold, her desire for the bone-chilling darkness of these nights and realisation rushed through her like water. Her mother was a spirit of Winter. It would explain everything.

Please join me.

Longing rushed through her and she almost ran to the cabin door. She retained enough thought to slow down and quietly open the locks and bolts to the door before she moved out into the snow. Her feet sank into the drift, the cold barely a concern. With light, fast steps she raced across the ground to stop before the figure that floated before her.

'Mother?'

'Yes.' The voice was the brittle chill of icicles and the tinkle of wind chimes in the breeze. 'You've grown.' Her fingers drifted across her skin, leaving a trail of cold that Rose was sure could have frozen any other.

'How?'

'Mother Winter chose me.' Blue eyes looked over the homestead. 'And I chose him.' A strange longing entered her voice. 'And our joining produced you.'

Bitterly cold arms wrapped about Rose and drew her into an embrace. Ice flowed across Rose's skin and yet she felt little pain.

'The last I saw you,' the musical voice drifted into her hair. 'You were small and full of warmth.'

'Why did you leave me?' Her voice was muffled against the frost-edge skin of Geada's shoulder. Once again Rose wondered how she could stand in the chill of her mother's arms. 'Why did my father not tell me?'

'My dear girl.' Another hug. 'You are mainly human and I am not.' Geada drew back and stared at Rose's tear-streaked face. 'Even if your gift held true, you could not stay with me.'

'My gift?' Rose felt like her world was spinning. Who was she if she wasn't human?

'My blessing then.' Gentle, icy fingers froze the tears on Rose's cheeks. 'The ice that laces your flesh.' A proud smile lit the spirit's face. 'The calling of your soul for Winter.' A gentle brush of ice that barely registered on skin traced lines across flesh. 'Not fully for the world of warmth.'

'I'm not human?'

'No, my snowdrop. You are a promise.'

'A promise?' Rose felt a fog begin to drift over her thoughts, the revelations of the night dulling her senses.

'To Winter, of course.' Geada drifted back from Rose and a sheet of black ice shimmered before her. In her darkened reflection Rose saw the pale cast to her skin and the ice gleaming in her dark hair. An image of chilling beauty and frost stood before her, an image that called achingly to her soul. 'Your grandmother knows this.' Rose glanced away from the image and back to the darkened house, echoes of her grandmother's warnings filling her head. 'She kept you from me and away from your destiny.'

'My destiny?'

'Yes, my sweet one.' A crystal laugh echoed over the clearing. 'You are the new Spirit of Winter.'

Chapter Sneak Peeks

If you enjoyed this book, and can't wait for the next instalment, check out these sample chapters from Amber Sky and Black Lotus.

THE BLACK LOTUS

15th June 1752

The floor was cold. That mundane thought floated through her mind as the deep dark of unconsciousness ebbed away. The unyielding surface sent small stabs of pain through her limbs as confusion set in. Her head felt heavy and somewhat hollow as she struggled to remember how she had fallen. She managed to blink; the simple task rendered difficult by the lassitude swamping her. As she struggled closer to full awareness, she became aware of something clasped in her hand. Its surface was smooth, shaped like a flower but, as she traced her fingers over it's surface, it seemed to spark a wary, almost sick sensation of worry.

"I think she's waking up,"

A voice, feminine and vaguely familiar, sounded close to her head. She tried to move, to turn her head to stare at the speaker but her body refused to cooperate, still caught in the spell of near insensibility. "Yes, I can see that," Another voice, male and disapproving, spoke from further away. "You need not sound so thrilled; I doubt she will welcome you when she opens her eyes."

"Oh, Hugh darling, how can you say that?" Petulant yet teasing notes flowed through the woman's light lilting speech and she longed to see the face that it belonged to. Those tones invoked cautious recognition, a recognition which did not bring her any sense of peace.

"Because it is the truth," The man shifted position and walked closer to her prone figure. "Why on earth did you do it?" The voice dropped lower, becoming accusatory in tone and timbre. She wondered at this, struggling with tattered threads of memory that refused to make sense.

"It solved a problem,"

"I beg to differ," He was stood over her now; she felt the tips of his toes against her side. "Do you think that Justin will thank you?"

Justin, that name caught at her mind, dragging it free from the sludge her memory had become. She knew that name, the feelings it provoked were soft and wondrous. Once again the memories fluttered close to the surface yet she was still not awake enough to make sense of it all

"He should," The voice argued, louder and less teasing than before, "This solves all," She felt the woman move, the edge of a skirt brushed against her side, and she wondered how long they were going to stand and argue over her.

"Really?" There was a bark of incredulous laughter. "Our Justin, who promised never to curse another," Her eyelids opened slightly, and she focused blearily on the rich brocade silk that tickled her nose. "Do you honestly think he would be happy that you damned someone else?" From her position on the floor, she could see the man's calves and a pair of silver buckled shoes.

"Yes Hugh," The skirt rustled as the woman stepped away from her side to argue with the man before her. "The chit is now safe. John will not be able to hurt her," Another memory tugged at the edges of her mind and this one sent a thrill of fear through her. "And Justin..," The woman laughed shortly, bitterly, "Justin will not spend the next fifty years in depression because he had to leave her,"

"Don't try to claim that you did this for him," The man knelt down now and she felt his hand close about her wrist. Her limited vision took in a rose pink satin frock coat and embroidered lavender waistcoat. "You did it for yourself. You've always felt like the youngest, and now you're not," His other hand reached down and settled in the small of her back. "Come on now Melissa, let me help you up," She did not question her name, for she remembered that at least.

With sure movements, he helped her to her feet. Her eyes opened fully, and she took in her surroundings. She was in a parlour, mahogany wainscoting covered the walls, and a thick blue rug topped the parquet floor. Several chairs stood around a card table in the corner of the room, and a fire was burning brightly in the hearth. Behind her lay a closed door and she could hear conversation and music from beyond. As the man guided her to a cushioned chair, she glanced up, taking in the extravagant clothing that seemed totally at odds with the serious cast marred his features.

"You'll be a little disorientated at first," She could see pity in his eyes, and she wondered at it. "It'll pass," He reached out to one of the small tables in the corner of the room and picked up a glass of amber liquid. "Take a snifter of that, it'll strengthen your nerves," The scent of brandy filled her nostrils, and she took a deep gulp. The liquid burned her throat as she swallowed and made her splutter. As she controlled her coughs, her eyes took in the form of the woman. Taller than her, the woman had blonde ringlets worn in an elaborate style and powdered. An expensive dress of dark blue brocade covered her form and blue eyes sparked with mischief or malice.

"What happened?" She asked, staring at the pair of them in confusion. "Did I faint?"

The man sighed and knelt down, staring at her with sorrowful eyes. "I'm sorry my dear, but," He held out his hand and she looked down at the small snuff box before her. Set into the lid was a black enamel locket in the shape of a lotus flower. The smooth planes of the bloom filled her vision, and she stared at it in utter shock. As horrified recognition raced through her; the man continued to speak. "You have one of these now and I'm so very sorry,"

It was then that she looked down, at the item clasped between her fingers. It was a lotus flower locket, a veritable twin to the one on the box. The sight of it finally sparked her memory and she remembered what it stood for. Her head snapped up and she stared at the blonde woman, hatred replacing shock as her mind finally filled in the gaps of her memory.

"You bitch."

AMBER SKY

*Within the coils of copper and brass,
there is a chance of freedom:*
ANONYMOUS WRITER (DATE UNKNOWN)

CHAPTER 1

It was November, and soot-laden fog obscured her progress as Taya strode along the busy street. A chill wind kept the smog moving and nipped at her exposed skin. She was grateful for the shifting whiteness: it kept away curious eyes, and gave her a sense of freedom. The Factory was ahead, belching clouds of smoke and steam into the air, choking the lines of workers that queued outside. She averted her eyes and kept going. Thoughts of the Factory led to thoughts of the mine, and she could not allow that. The work site fell behind her as she began to move uphill, away from the choking smog of the Factory District, and towards the Mercantile District. The traffic thinned out as her feet carried her through the cold, whispering quiet. The crowds were lighter here and better dressed. In contrast to their well-heeled looks, Taya looked like an old sack. Several threadbare garments covered her body, and a moth-eaten, woollen hat was jammed down on her chestnut coloured hair. Her boots were held together with twine, and stuffed with rags to keep the cold out. Despite her efforts to layer her ragged clothing, the wind still found its way to her skin, making her shiver. As she headed into the district, the fog-shrouded her from prying eyes and made her progress easier. Moving along the well-paved roads of the merchant district with the elusiveness of a wild thing, she avoided the few merchants that braved the cold, speeding up as she reached her destination.

The house was built from white stone, now discoloured from the ubiquitous soot. On the faded cherry-red door, a brass knocker in the shape of a lion warned her off with what she fancied was a contemptuous gaze. For a long moment, she stared at the wood, wondering at the wisdom of what she was attempting. Lars and Cody could have been wrong, and this trip could easily land her in the cells. As the ever-present wind chapped her lips, she mustered her resolve. All other options had been exhausted, and this was all she had left. Taking a deep breath, she grasped the knocker with one shaking hand before letting it fall. For several moments, she waited on the doorstep, shifting uneasily from one foot to the other, nervous beyond thought.

The door creaked open, and a maid stared down at her with unconcealed distaste. Taya nervously wet her lips and opened her mouth to speak.

"No beggars," The maid spoke first, her voice shrill with strident condemnation, as she took in Tay's attire. Confident in her dismissal, she moved to close the door.

"No, wait," Tay placed her foot in the hall, and leant forward. The maid stopped moving, distaste turning into shock. "I need to speak to Darius..." Despite her best efforts, Tay's voice still shook. "Please," The woman stared down at her with disbelief, incredulous at her audacity to ask to see the Master's son.

"I don't think so," The woman began pushing the door shut, physically moving Tay's fragile frame with its wooden weight. Tay held her ground, trying to keep the door open.

"Please..." She pleaded once more, her voice echoing loudly in the hallway. Panic thrummed through her, mindful of the spectacle she was creating. One complaint from any of the people on the street behind her and the guards would come. "I need to see him," It was a desperate, yearning plea, yet the maid was having none of it. The door jammed against her toes, and she winced. The maid was winning the battle, her far stronger, well-fed bulky frame inching Tay closer to the street, with each movement of the door.

"What's going on?" A male voice echoed across the hall, and the maid stopped.

"It's this beggar, Sir," The woman held the door steady, as she turned to face the speaker. "She wishes to talk to you," Her voice was sneering, only slightly mollified by deference to her master.

"Let me see," The man walked forward, and the maid reluctantly released her hold on the door. Tay's eyes roved across a well-tailored, dark blue suit which framed a lean body, and a cane of some dark wood laid carelessly in his slender elegant fingers. Casting her gaze upwards, she stared directly into a pair of deep blue eyes, which were alight with interest.

"I need to see you, Darius," She appealed directly to him, holding his gaze with silent entreaty. She ignored the scandalised tut of the maid beside her, as she took a step forward. "It's important."

Darius thought for a moment before he nodded. "Let her in," He said to the maid, stepping back along the hall. With a look of shock on her features, the woman stepped away from the door and let Taya into the house.